PRAISE FOR

Beach Rental

DOUBLE WINNER IN THE 2012 GDRWA BOOKSELLERS
BEST AWARD

FINALIST IN THE 2012 GAYLE WILSON AWARD OF
EXCELLENCE

FINALIST IN THE 2012 PUBLISHED MAGGIE AWARD
FOR EXCELLENCE

"No author can come close to capturing the awe-inspiring essence of the North Carolina coast like Greene. Her debut novel seamlessly combines hope, love and faith, like the female equivalent of Nicholas Sparks. Her writing is meticulous and so finely detailed you'll hear the gulls overhead and the waves crashing onto shore. Grab a hanky, bury your toes in the sand and get ready to be swept away with this unforgettable beach read." —*RT Book Reviews 4.5 stars TOP PICK*

Beach Winds

FINALIST IN THE 2014 OKRWA INTERNATIONAL
DIGITAL AWARDS

FINALIST IN THE 2014 WISRA WRITE TOUCH
READERS' AWARD

"Greene's follow up to Beach Rental is exquisitely written with lots of emotion and tugging on the heartstrings. Returning to Emerald Isle is like a warm reunion with an old friend and readers will be inspired by the captivating story where we excitedly get to meet new characters and reconnect with a few familiar faces, too. The author's perfect prose highlights family relationships which we may find similar to our own and will have you dreaming of strolling along the shore to rediscover yourself in no time at all. This novel will have one wondering about faith, hope and courage and you may be lucky enough to gain all three by the time Beach Winds last page is read." —*RT Book Reviews 4.5 stars TOP PICK*

Kincaid's Hope

FINALIST IN THE 2013 GDRWA BOOKSELLERS' BEST AWARD

FINALIST IN THE 2013 GAYLE WILSON AWARD OF EXCELLENCE

"A quiet, backwater town is the setting for intrigue, deception, and betrayal in this exceptional sophomore offering. Greene's ability to pull the reader into the story and emotionally invest them in the characters makes this book a great read." —*RT Book Reviews, 4 STARS*

The Happiness In Between

"The Happiness In Between overflows with the warmth, healing, and hope Greene fans know to expect in her uplifting stories." *—Christine Nolfi, author of Sweet Lake*

Wildflower Heart

"…An affecting and emotionally resonant tale of love, loss, and the possibility of second chances that's bolstered by a winsome heroine, well-drawn supporting characters, and a nuanced story full of surprising twists and turns."*—Kirkus Reviews*

"Beautifully crafted, Wildflower Heart is an emotionally powerful novel about healing past wounds, and starting over. With the lush Virginia countryside as a backdrop, Greene explores the family secrets of a stoic father and his grieving daughter with heart and authenticity—and with surprising twists—that will have readers turning the pages long into the night." *—Christine Nolfi, bestselling author of the Sweet Lake series*

Wildflower Hope

"In her second Wildflower novel, Greene masterfully peels back the hidden layers of Kara Hart's grief, dependency, and self-doubt to unveil a heartwarming tale of love and forgiveness. Set in the lush Virginia countryside, Wildflower Hope is an inspirational story of leaving the past behind and seeing the possibilities of the future."—*Bette Lee Crosby, USA Today bestselling author of Emily, Gone*

"Kara Hart is at a crossroads in her life—grieving the loss of her father, rehabbing a house for use as a creative retreat, hoping for love, and trying to move past a betrayal by her friend Victoria. Grace Greene does an artful job taking us along on Kara's journey, weaving in moments of her life, both past and present. Fans of the first book in the series will love jumping back into the comforting world of Cub Creek, but new readers won't have any problem picking up the threads of the story. Reading a novel by Grace Greene is like being wrapped in a blanket of love and healing and Wildflower Hope delivers on all counts. Highly recommended!" —*Karen McQuestion, bestselling author of Hello Love*

WILDFLOWER CHRISTMAS

A Wildflower House Novella

The Wildflower House Series, Book 3

BOOKS BY GRACE GREENE

Emerald Isle, North Carolina Novels

Beach Rental
Beach Winds
Beach Wedding
"Beach Towel" (A Short Story)
Beach Christmas *(Christmas Novella)*
Beach Walk *(Christmas Novella)*
Clair *(Beach Brides Novella Series)*

Virginia Country Roads Novels

Kincaid's Hope
A Stranger in Wynnedower
Cub Creek
Leaving Cub Creek

Stand-Alone Novels

The Happiness In Between
The Memory of Butterflies

Wildflower House Novels

Wildflower Heart
Wildflower Hope
Wildflower Christmas *(A Wildflower Novella)*

WILDFLOWER CHRISTMAS

A Wildflower House Novella

The Wildflower House Series, Book 3

By Grace Greene

Kersey Creek Books

Text copyright © 2019 by Grace Greene
All rights reserved.

Published by Kersey Creek Books

ISBN-13: 978-0-9996180-7-3 (eBook)
ISBN-13: 978-0-9996180-6-6 (Print IS)
ISBN-13: 978-0-9996180-5-9 (Large Print IS)

Cover design by Grace Greene
Printed in the United States of America

Wildflower Christmas is dedicated to my family and friends—those I know, those I've yet to meet, and the friends I'll never meet face-to-face. You are all essential to the foundation and framework of my life and memories.

Wildflower Christmas is dedicated to the readers who encourage me in this writing endeavor. You are a priceless gift. I write these books for you.

For all the books I've had the opportunity to write and share—from Beach Rental *to* Wildflower Christmas *and beyond—I thank God for this blessing.*

WELCOME TO THE WILDFLOWER HOUSE SERIES

~ An Introduction ~

In *Wildflower Heart*, Kara Hart, a thirty-two-year-old widow, moves to Wildflower House with her father who plans to renovate the old mansion. In *Wildflower Hope*, Kara takes her father's dream of renovating the old mansion and makes it her own.

A wildflower must bloom where it finds itself and Kara chooses to do exactly that at Wildflower House, putting her grief behind her and moving forward with renovations to turn the old mansion into a creative retreat and event space.

In *Wildflower Christmas*, Kara is looking forward to a quiet holiday—just like the ones she's always known—but this year, instead of celebrating the holidays with her father in the city, she's at Wildflower House and she's alone. Kara is okay with a low-key Christmas because after hosting the hectic first official event at Wildflower House she's ready for rest and relaxation before January arrives and the final renovations begin.

But fate—with a heaping dose of Christmas spirit—intervenes as the people now in Kara's life show up to celebrate. Some need favors and others have special gifts, and if Kara can up her holiday game, she may find new traditions she can build on for the future.

WILDFLOWER CHRISTMAS

Prologue

I'd first seen Wildflower House in the spring when the locals still called it the old Forster place. I'd grown up in Richmond, but had never been to Louisa County or heard of a place called Cub Creek until my dad said he was retiring and moving there. It was, according to him, an integral part of his retirement plan.

Retirement? A plan? He was only sixty. He'd built his tire and automotive business from the ground up and had poured his energy and dedication into it for most of his life. That business had been his baby—in many ways, more than I'd been.

But we know what we know, and that's what we tend to pass on to our children. Dad hadn't always been physically or emotionally present, but he'd been the best father he knew how to be—and he'd always come to my rescue when I needed him the most.

For the past two years, I'd been living with my father as I recovered from my own disasters. I had learned for myself how vulnerable a person could become, even overnight. Had that happened to my father? Was someone attempting to take advantage of him?

I went to see the property for myself. I found a vacant, decaying Victorian mansion in the middle of badly overgrown grounds surrounded by dense forest. But the open, sunny backyard sloping down to the creek was covered in vibrant masses of wildflowers. The colors, the wild and stunning shapes and variety, had overwhelmed me, jolting me out of a doldrum I hadn't known I was mired in. In that moment, I decided to move there with Dad, at least long enough to help him settle in before I left to reestablish my own independent life. I was thirty-two and mostly well by then. It was time for me to be on my own again.

So we moved to Wildflower House last April. For me, spring became a time of healing from my past sorrows, especially as my father began sharing secrets from his childhood. With the missing pieces finally filling in the picture of our lives, our relationship was improving.

Until Dad died in June.

Losing him devastated me. Summer ushered in grief but also fear—the nearly paralyzing fear of having to make decisions alone, and probably failing. As summer transitioned into autumn, my heart finally allowed a lifetime of memories with my dad—and even the memories of my mom, who'd died years before—to displace my stubborn mourning, giving me emotional permission to jump full force into turning Wildflower House into a creative retreat and event space. The renovation wasn't complete yet, but the main floor—with its wide hallways, high ceilings, wood paneling, and huge rooms—was done.

The old house had bloomed after Thanksgiving with the help of my new friends, and an old one, Victoria, as we prepared for our first official event, the Ladies' Auxiliary Holiday Open House. It was held in early December and went brilliantly. After the craziness of the event, and before the last of the renovations began in January, I wanted a break and a rest. I thought I could coast into a laid-back holiday—a quiet, solitary Christmas like the ones I'd always known.

In fact, a quiet, solitary Christmas was all I'd *ever* known—*until I arrived at Wildflower House.*

CHAPTER ONE

Monday, December 9 ~

Sixteen Days Until Christmas

Wildflower House had been the perfect event space for the Ladies' Auxiliary Holiday Open House held on Saturday evening. The members had decorated the entire first floor, including the front porch, which was festooned with lights, evergreen boughs, and holly. Many of the decorations had been created by the auxiliary members who were displaying their crafts and who'd also provided tables laden with all sorts of cakes, candies, and hor d'oeuvres. Even nature had cooperated, providing polite flurries of snow that added to the holiday feel without impeding traffic or attendance.

Two days later, on Monday, I was still enjoying the afterglow of the good will exchanged between and among so many people. Most of the attendees had been strangers to me, but they'd introduced themselves, and I'd been as friendly and gracious as I could. How would I ever remember all those new names and faces? If I ran into them while in Mineral or in the larger town of Louisa, would they expect me to recognize them? I shook my head. I'd certainly try, but in recent years I'd become accustomed to a smaller, more isolated world.

At the end of the event, the auxiliary members had taken most of their crafts and decorations home while they had the help of their families. Some had returned today to retrieve the remaining decorations. As they thanked me all over again for hosting the event at Wildflower House, I imagined how my stoic dad would've reacted to all this and to the changes I'd made. He would've loved it. Every bit of it. But what he would've loved the most was that his younger sister, my Aunt Laura, was now in my life. That would've made him over-the-moon happy. For me, it was bittersweet to witness how narrowly they'd missed meeting each other as adults after a separation of almost forty-seven years.

And then there was Will Mercer. I watched as he carried a box filled with sparkly garland. It tickled his face, and I wanted to laugh but kept my amusement contained within a poorly concealed smirk.

"I'll be right back," he said and exited via the front door.

Will's broad-shouldered, rough-looking exterior contrasted with his good-natured support and a surprisingly romantic nature. He worked for Mitchell's Lawn and Landscaping. He'd come to Wildflower House for a landscaping job and had made himself an important part of my life. Perhaps an essential part. As I thought of him, my fingers moved in the air, wanting to touch his dark hair and reexperience his vivid blue eyes meeting mine. A perilous blue. But there was nothing dangerous about Will. His manner could be abrupt, but his heart was open and honest, and it was mine.

Among the auxiliary members who'd returned today to take down the remaining decorations and craft displays was Sue Deale. She was something of a mover-shaker busybody, but with a heart of gold. She insisted I keep the two decorated trees in the front rooms, some of the mantel decorations, and the paper snowflakes hanging from the foyer ceiling.

"Trust me, Kara. You won't regret it," Sue said. "You're lucky. Your Christmas decorations are already done!" Then she hustled the last of the auxiliary members—including Aunt Laura—out the front door, everyone's arms filled with boxes and bags of decorations. Sue Deale gave me a wink and a wave as she stepped out and the storm door closed behind her.

Laura would be back too. She and I had plans for

this afternoon.

My dad, Henry Lange, had spent most of his life trying to find his younger twin siblings, but he'd never succeeded. He'd only been gone about four months when Aunt Laura had introduced herself to me at the first *unofficial* event held at Wildflower House—a book club meeting back in October. It was stunning to consider that if Sue Deale hadn't convinced me to host that book club meeting Laura might have approached me eventually, but being so shy, it would have taken her a lot longer—maybe too long.

Will walked back inside. His arms were free now. He took the opportunity to drape a stolen bit of garland around my neck and to kiss me. He said, "I'll be tied up with the Slocum job for a couple of days. He's anxious to get it finished before his family begins arriving for a long holiday visit."

He touched my cheek, pressed his lips to mine again, but too briefly, and then said, "I'll get this last box out to Sue and take off. If you have any jobs you need done before the holidays, make a list and I'll handle it when I get back."

"A list?"

"Mom has a list, and my grandmother has a list. I hope you will too. Makes me feel useful." He touched my hair and my cheek. "See you soon, Kara." And he left.

Solitude had never been a problem for me, but with the departure of the ladies and now Will, too, I felt a sharp pang of loneliness. I was glad that Laura would be staying to visit for a little while this afternoon.

I sank into Dad's chair in the sitting room and stared at the tree. The angel topper nearly reached the high ceiling. The tree was garbed in evergreen garland, holly sprigs, and cherry picks. Shiny ribbons and glass ornaments completed the outfit. It made me think of designer-decorated trees one might see in the display window of a high-end department store. Wildflower House was grand, too, but for me, for the holidays, such excessive decorations felt like overkill. Yet beyond the wide opening of the sitting room and the large, open foyer was the parlor with its own equally elegant tree. And across that vista of ceiling between the rooms, numerous snowflakes and other seasonal paper cuttings were hung. They were all merry reminders of the open house. But now it was just me, with nothing planned for the remainder of December. I was ready to hibernate, not celebrate. The next stage of renovation would begin in January, and I wanted this peaceful interlude to think, to be sure I was on the right track with this house and my business.

A quiet Christmas seemed perfect for that.

I peeked out the window and saw Laura, Sue, and some of the others still out there chatting. Goodness, but they never ran out of conversation.

Laura and I had things to discuss, too, which would likely lead to other, more awkward topics. It was hard to know exactly what and how much to share with my gentle aunt. I'd fix us a snack. A little iced tea and a couple of cookies couldn't hurt.

On my way to the kitchen, I paused to adjust a ribbon on the tree and to tweak the garland on the fireplace mantel. Yes, the decorations were unnecessary, but they were pretty. And it was nice to have them already done without effort or decision on my part. This year, being mostly on my own, I wouldn't have bothered.

Certainly, Dad and I never had. Through my growing up years, we'd stuck with the obligatory tree and a few presents. It was as if my father—a single parent, and a brilliant, driven man who'd built a thriving business from the ground up—had never learned the art of celebrating holidays. His childhood home had been a grim place, and it had become even grimmer after his mother died and his younger siblings disappeared. Dad hadn't learned the joy of or appreciation for Christmas from his father, and thus he hadn't passed it on to me.

As I poured us each an iced tea with slices of orange and apple floating on top, I considered the two weeks between now and Christmas Day. Two weeks and two days, to be precise. It would be quiet here at Wildflower

House. Perhaps my aunt would join me for a meal on Christmas Eve? Or I might join the Albers family for Christmas dinner. They lived just a walk away on the far side of Cub Creek. Mel and her daughter, Nicole, would welcome me, and it would be fun to spend time with a child at Christmas. Maddie Lyn, Mel Albers's granddaughter, was only five.

Would Seth come home from Los Angeles for the holidays? Not long ago, I'd thought Seth and I were sweethearts and would be building a future together. But when Seth had accepted a new job in LA, things had changed. It had taken that distance between us for me to realize that Seth and I were better as friends than as a couple. And that understanding had opened the way for Will and me to grow closer.

If Mel did invite me, I could bring a covered dish like in one of those movies where happy neighbors share casseroles and friendship, and their troubles are no bigger than hangnails.

I liked that idea.

In fact, maybe Will would invite me to spend time with his family? I already knew his sister, Britt. Sooner or later I should meet his mom. This might be the right season for that too.

Laura called out, "Kara?"

"I'm in the kitchen."

She was tall and thin, without the robustness or confidence of my father, yet there was something about the shape of her jaw, or maybe in the set of her cheekbones, that reminded me of Dad. I had my father's hazel eyes and my mother's dark hair. Laura's hair was a mix of gray and light brown, and her eyes were a faded blue, but it was more than the color of her hair or her eyes that set her apart from us. When I looked at Aunt Laura, I saw gentleness and timidity, very unlike Dad and me.

Laura's whole aspect was so different from the steady, solid demeanor of my father. As his younger sister, she had his look but in a slender, more fragile edition. Laura and Lewis had been given away—adopted—when they were hardly more than toddlers. It had been their sudden, unexpected departure that had prompted Dad to run away from home as a teenager, to find his own way and eventually begin his business.

"Sorry to be so long," Laura said. "The ladies are gone now." She gave me a sidelong glance, smiling. "That Will Mercer—he's such a nice young man."

I let her remark pass.

Laura noted my silence and laughed. The sound was light and airy, and gentle. Everything about Aunt Laura was genteel and careful. "At any rate, the others are heading out now. Going to lunch together."

"I hope I'm not spoiling any plans for you?"

"Not at all. I'm eager to go over the DNA results." She shrugged. "Silly, I know. If there was anything in the report that would lead us to Lewis, you would've told me right away."

"True, but remember, Laura, the lack of positive results doesn't mean your twin brother isn't alive and living happily with a wife and a houseful of kids and grandkids. If they haven't taken a DNA test like this and shared the results, then we simply wouldn't know. Don't give up."

Laura shrugged. "A houseful of family sounds wonderful." She shook off her imaginings. "I don't have much hope we'll find him. It's been too long, and I remember so little. Lewis and I were three, about to turn four. I'm fifty now. That's a long time for trails to go cold, for people to get old and ill, and for memories to fade."

She pressed her hands against mine. "I missed finding my older brother, Henry, but I found you, and I'm grateful. Yet even that was by chance. I think of the efforts I made when I first returned to Louisa County—to no avail."

Laura smiled. "It took a miracle to bring us together, Kara. Maybe a couple of miracles. First, Nicole speaking about women's entrepreneurship at our Ladies' Auxiliary meeting. She talked about Kara Hart and her father, Henry. Not Lange. Second, if I hadn't been on Sue's cleanup crew after the meeting, I wouldn't have learned that you were a widow and that your father wasn't Henry Hart, but was Henry *Lange*. Suppose I'd missed the auxiliary meeting that day? I would never have found you."

"Dad always wondered what happened to his younger siblings, but he wasn't able to find answers. I'm so glad you showed up on my doorstep and so sorry you and Dad missed finding each other by such a small window of time."

I hugged her. "We'll either find Lewis or we won't, but we'll keep trying, and I'm so glad to have you in my life." I kept my hands on her arms. "Come sit down with me at the computer, and we'll go through the data the DNA company sent." As we walked down the hallway, I added, "And if you ever decide to get a computer yourself, you let me know. I'd be delighted to help you set it up and learn how to use it."

We carried our tea to the workroom, situated in an almost overlooked space between the parlor, the foyer, and the grand stairs. It was my office and my creative haven too. A long table held my computer and office stuff like pens and tape and such, and I'd taped a hand-drawn map of Wildflower House and the immediate property on the wall. Working in the heart of the house and surrounded by my plans for it kept me centered.

Laura and I sat together and reviewed the results of

both DNA tests, but the data was almost too detailed. We were just hoping to find evidence of Lewis or his descendants. I tried to keep the conversation light, but Laura's disappointment was palpable. We were each other's only family connections, except for some distant possible cousins.

"Really distant," I emphasized.

"Perhaps they are our mother's relations."

"Mother?"

"Our birth mother, of course. Your grandmother on your father's side—old Mr. Lange's wife. I don't know her name or anything about her family. Do you?"

I shook my head, thinking hard. Had Dad ever mentioned his mother's name? If he had, I couldn't recall it. "No, but I believe Dad mentioned they're interred in a cemetery in the Mineral area. Even if there are no grave markers, there are surely records of who's buried there. If we can't chase it down before Christmas, we'll go together after."

She sighed. "So close. Yet they might as well be on the moon."

I looked down. Laura was wearing sturdy, no-nonsense walking shoes.

"Grab your coat. Let's take a walk. We'll enjoy the fresh air and afternoon sun."

She looked surprised.

"You haven't seen much of the Wildflower property, have you?"

"The yard? I love what the landscaping accomplished. Things were sadly overgrown before you and Henry went to work on it."

"You've missed seeing the nooks. Mary and Rob Forster created them."

"Nooks?"

"Small spots in the fringes of the woods for resting and thinking. I'll show you my favorite. It was Dad's favorite, too, and I don't mean in recent times. I'm talking about when he was a boy. He'd walk up the creek path to engage with the family who lived here before the Forsters. Coming here was his escape."

Laura's surprise had given way to interest and now settled on confusion.

"There's a creek path?"

I said softly, "It follows Cub Creek from here to the old Lange property where your family lived."

She whispered, "The Lange property?"

"The house is in shambles. It fell in on itself many years ago."

She all but breathed the words, "It's still there?"

"You don't know about it?"

"No. Remember, I didn't grow up here. I knew my birth family had lived somewhere in Louisa County, but I grew up in New Mexico. I had no connections in this area. After I moved back, I made inquiries, but no one knew anything." She touched my sleeve. "Kara, even if it's just a grown-over debris pile in the woods, I'd like to see it."

"I'll take you there, but it's a sad place."

Laura was already on her feet, ignoring my warning. "I'll grab my coat and scarf."

I nodded, but I wasn't sure about this. I didn't like that twisted wreck of a house or the feel of neglect or the overwhelming despair it instilled in me. That said, how much of my discomfort with the homesite came from Dad's retelling of his young life there? Laura would know only what I chose to tell her.

Taking my coat from the closet, I joined my aunt in the kitchen. Her face was glowing. I had no good news to share with her, but I did have information from Dad out of those last conversations we'd shared. I could choose what to tell his baby sister. She was eager to know. Who could blame her? It was her history too.

"As a matter of fact, while we're out there, I'll cut a few snippets of holly for decoration." I grabbed the garden scissors from the kitchen drawer, the magnet spot where such things always ended up.

Laura smiled, showing surprise. "The auxiliary members didn't leave enough decorations behind today?"

"This is for something special. Something we

overlooked."

Snug against the December chill in our coats and scarves, Laura and I paused at the medallion garden with the statue in the center surrounded by plantings. The azaleas were already in place, but Will would add flowers in the spring. He'd installed colored spotlights here to highlight the central figure—a girl reaching out to birds and butterflies. It always gave me a sense of peace to see her poised here with the sweep of the lawn behind her as it sloped down to the creek.

We would keep those spotlights permanently in place, along with the light strings Will had run through the tree branches along the path to the gray stone carriage house.

Laura and I crossed the lawn to the left side of the yard and followed the earthen walkway beside the tree line down toward the creek. When we were two-thirds of the way along, I stopped and pointed out the stone steps, barely visible between the evergreen growth. We stood at the top of the steps, and I put my hand on her arm.

"These leaves on the stone steps look pretty, but they can be slippery."

She smiled at me. "I've been walking for almost fifty years now. I can handle it."

"Good. Then *you* can catch *me* if I slip."

"I will, indeed."

It was so odd to be reminded that my aunt was ten years younger than my father. She was only fifty. And yet, by comparison, Dad at sixty had seemed so much more robust. We walked down the steps, and Laura swept the dry pool and the gazing ball and bench with a glance. I kept my hand on her arm.

She said, "It's so private and tranquil. I'll bet it's beautiful in the spring when these trees flower."

"It is." I gestured at the view before us, saying, "It didn't look like this when Dad was a kid. This was a vantage point from which he watched the family who lived here until he finally found the guts to speak to them. They treated him kindly. It was a place to go when he didn't want to be home. A place where people asked about his grades and paid him to rake leaves and gave him snacks."

We stopped at the foot of the steps. The cast-iron bench was to our right, and the dry fishpond was to the left. Autumn's cast-off leaves had carpeted the stones and earth. I pointed at the gazing ball on its pedestal.

"That's why we call it the Gazing Ball Grotto."

"Nice. You said there are more of these nooks?"

"There are. This is the largest." I shivered. "It's chilly down here, isn't it? Let's keep moving."

We climbed back to the open yard area and walked down nearer the creek, where I pointed out the paths. "To the right is the path that leads to the wooden bridge and a distance farther to the Alberses' home." I pointed to our left. "That way goes to the Lange property. No one lives there, and hasn't for a long time. The land actually adjoins the Wildflower property, but it's quite a walk, as you're about to see."

We followed the path without much talk. Will and his landscaping crew had widened the trail, making it better underfoot without infringing on the wild feel. The sun in its winter blue sky peeked through the mostly bare branches overhead, and alongside the path the small evergreens and hollies had their time to shine. The creek sang its music as it flowed along next to us. I felt pride. I hadn't created this, but I'd tried to conserve it while making it an enjoyable walk for the guests who'd eventually visit here. I raised my face to the sun—and promptly stumbled on a root. I recovered quickly and paid closer attention to where I was putting my feet.

Laura said, "I see lots of beautiful holly trees with red berries. Do you want to grab some cuttings?"

I shook my head. "Let's do it on the way back."

The farther we walked, the heavier the pall grew around us. Or was it just me feeling edgy? I glanced at Laura's face. She looked serene, with eagerness brightening her eyes. Laura was seeking a connection to her first years—I understood that. She must be hoping that something would strike a familiar chord.

Where we left the path and headed inland, the trail hadn't been cleared. I hadn't had this part improved because I didn't want to encourage future guests to visit the ruins. There were too many hazards. An old well, for one, plus innumerable rotting boards, shards of broken glass, and rusty nails.

We'd already had hard frosts, so snakes weren't a worry, but thorns were a year-round hazard, in addition to those small bits of debris from the house that had been scattered about by decades of storms.

"Wait," I said. I moved the sticker bush branches aside. "Go ahead. It's just past these trees."

Laura stared. "I think I see a roof. Collapsed?"

"Yes. Watch your step, please. Nothing has changed since old Mr. Lange—sorry, that would be your father—passed. Before that even, because I don't think he was living here in his last years. Nothing, except what nature has wrought upon it. And nature has not been kind."

I stared, dismayed at the state of the old house. "Take your time, Laura, but watch out for broken glass and whatever else. And stay away from the well." I stepped back to give her space.

Many months ago, I'd sat on the fallen tree beside my father as he told me about his dreadful childhood. Now I was sitting here watching my aunt pick her way back from examining the crumpled house debris. A pine tree had fallen across what was left of the house, probably during one of the late-summer storms that had thundered through this past September, so it was even worse than I recalled. For me, there seemed a feeling to the air itself, as if memories had been held here. Bad memories. Bad acts.

Dad hadn't had the heart or the will to clear it. I, too, had delayed out of a silly, superstitious feeling that leaving it intact might bring the last sibling home.

We'd waited. And what had waiting gotten us? For instance, if Dad had opened up to me sooner, or if he'd lived longer, I could've asked him about his mother, her name and so on. I would've known the answer. I would've had that information to share with Laura.

Maybe it was time to move forward.

Laura knelt and picked up a shiny bit of paper. She held it almost absentmindedly, and after a few minutes she walked back to where I waited.

"It feels sad, doesn't it?" she asked.

"For me too." I squinted at the paper in her hand. "What's that?"

She held it out. "A candy wrapper."

I took it from her. "Looks pretty fresh. Wonder how it got here?"

"Probably kids."

"Of course. Sure." But it made me uneasy. Did this decay, this aura of loss and abandonment, attract some people? Also, it might be an injury and insurance hazard. Someone could injure themselves stepping on a nail or a broken piece of window glass. Or a teenager might pry the cement lid off the well and fall in.

I wished my brain hadn't gone down that road. I shivered, saying, "Maybe it's time to clear it all out."

"What will you do with the property? I presume it belongs to you?"

"It does. Dad kept the taxes paid but couldn't bring himself to do more with it." I would not repeat Dad's fear that their father might have harmed the twins himself and perhaps had buried them here. There was no decent reason to plant that image in Laura's head. "But I don't like the idea of kids, or anyone else, making it a hangout of some kind. Anyone who'd hang out here would have to be troubled."

"I don't have any memory of this place. Not a shred."

"It was long ago. You and Lewis were very young. This all looked different back then. When you were here, your mom was alive. It wasn't until after she died that things went from bad to worse for Mr. Lange and you three children. In fact, to be fair, I suspect Mr. Lange found it difficult, maybe impossible, to care for such small children, twins, on his own after his wife, your mother, died."

Laura sighed loudly. "You said before that when Henry was a child, he spent as much time as possible away from this place? He preferred Wildflower House to his own home? How very sad."

"Dad said the day he came home from school and learned you and Lewis were gone, his father refused to discuss it with him. Dad worried . . . so much. But he had no power to do anything. It was then that he decided to leave. He was barely fourteen, so he couldn't leave right away, but by the time he was fifteen, he was working odd jobs in Richmond. He passed for older, he worked, and he succeeded."

"I wish I remembered him other than as a vague figure, that I'd known him as an adult. If I'd realized the connection sooner . . . that he was a Lange, the same as me. It's strange to think that I returned here more than twenty years ago. Henry returned this year. And still we missed each other." She put her hand to her chest. "It makes me wonder if that near miss will also happen with Lewis. If he's still alive." She shook her head. "Lots of ifs, but I don't want to miss seeing him again too. Not if I can avoid it."

I put my hand on hers. "If he's still alive, there's a good chance we'll find him. So much information is available now that wasn't when Dad and you were looking. Dad went to Richmond. You ended up in New

Mexico." I laughed but in a wry manner. "The people who raised Lewis probably moved somewhere else too. We'll continue doing what we can to find him and hope we'll be fortunate."

We began the trek back. I shoved the crumpled candy wrapper into my pocket.

It was only a bit of litter, but its presence unnerved me. How would anyone know they were trespassing out here? There were no fences, no signs.

I would discuss options with Will.

As we walked back along the path, I tried to lift our moods by shifting our attention to the holly branches laden with red berries and Christmas preparations. As I added to the cuttings, I asked, "Do you have plans for Christmas?"

She shook her head. "Christmas? I usually have Christmas dinner with one of my friends from church. Lots of us outlive our husbands, or sometimes just our marriages. There are no children, or they live far away. There are lots of lonely people in this world."

"Well, if you find yourself at loose ends, I'd love to have you join me. We'll keep it quiet and simple. It will be a low-key holiday for me. It's been a hectic, emotional year, and the coming year will be crazy, too, with the renovations and the business actually opening."

"I'd love to share Christmas with you. I haven't spent a holiday with family since my husband died."

"Excellent. It's a date. Christmas dinner."

Laura smiled and nodded. "Let me know what time to arrive and what I should bring."

~~~~

I called Will that night. I wanted to get his thoughts on the candy wrapper at the Lange homesite.

With a fluffy blanket wrapped around me like a huge shawl, I sat on the back-porch steps. It was a cold night, but the air was crisp, and the stars seemed magnified. The air and the view cleared my head and relaxed me.

"What do you think, Will? The trash only tells me that someone has been there. Likely passing through. But it feels like a dangerous place for teens to hang out or for strangers to use as a cut-through. The creek path looks so inviting now. I feel odd thinking any stranger might come strolling out of the woods."

"Have you given more thought to hauling the debris out of there?"

"Dad had his reasons for leaving it as it was. Maybe I've been a little superstitious about it too."

"You have Laura now. Maybe it's time."

"Thank you, Will. I'll see you tomorrow?"

"I'll check out the area and then come by to see you." He added, "Maybe it's a good idea to keep the doors locked, and not just at night."

"I suppose that's smart."

"Just thinking realistically."

We said good night in unison, laughed together, and then disconnected.

I felt a little sad. As if keeping my doors locked represented a change—and not a good one. Maybe a reasonable one. But . . .

One thing I'd noticed about Wildflower House—or maybe it was something that came with living in the country—was that if the front door was open, leaving only an unlocked screen door or storm door as a barrier to the world, the people one knew tended to just walk in after a quick knock and yell. Nicole certainly did. Sue Deale and others had too. No one ever rang the doorbell—almost as if they thought it might be rude in some odd way to suggest the formality was necessary between friends.

Maybe I was okay with my friends walking in. Hannah Cooper, a local artist who worked with clay, and whose skills I hoped to leverage for future visitors who were interested in such types of creative activities, had advised keeping the metaphorical doors open to see what might walk into my life.

Likely, she hadn't intended her advice to be taken quite so literally.

CHAPTER TWO

Tuesday, December 10 ~

Fifteen Days Until Christmas

"Kara?"

"Will? I'm back here," I yelled as I put the pitcher in the fridge.

Will walked so quietly up the hallway that I knew he'd removed his work shoes. He was thoughtful that way.

"The front door wasn't locked," he said.

"No. I was expecting you."

He came close and hugged me, kissing me but breaking off too soon. I'd told him I wanted to take things slowly, but it was obvious that we were both unsure of what that meant and kept bumping into that boundary. I appreciated that Will was respectful of my wishes, but I was going to have to find a way to commit to Will—or choose not to—because this middle-of-the-road stuff was for the birds.

Perhaps sensing my emotional struggle, Will

27

stepped away, accepted a glass of iced tea from me, and said, "I checked the Lange property. Found a few marks that might be shoeprints. Nothing definitive, and I'd guess there's nothing to worry about."

I frowned. "A hiker might cut through, I suppose. Do you think this was a one-time passing through?"

He shook his head. "I saw no signs of an overnight stay or repeated visits. It's the wrong time of year anyway for people to be hanging out in the woods without shelter. Even teenagers looking for privacy would likely prefer something with walls." He shook his head. "Probably just someone who came upon it by chance and kept going."

The path began in my backyard. Down by the creek, of course. A small distance from my home. But still. I felt exposed in a way I hadn't before.

Will put his arms around me. "No worries, Kara. Probably a hunter or hiker passing through. If you do want to clear out the wreckage, we can get a truck partway back there coming from the main road, but unless you want to improve the road, it will be a largely manual job, and probably best undertaken in early spring."

I put my hand on his arm. "Come spring, then."

"And then what?"

"What?"

"Just saying that you're going to have a vacant lot out there. It's nice acreage, especially since you own that property and this. Give it some thought over the winter."

"Dad felt the need to wait. I did too." I sighed. "Sometimes it's hard letting go. Even of things we don't like or want."

In response, he tightened his arms around me, and as if on cue we shared a kiss. Just as I was wondering if I should, or even if I could, disengage, Will did it for me. Without loosening his arms, he stepped back a fraction, just enough to communicate the change to me, and he touched my cheek and my hair to tell me he regretted having to do it.

I'd suffered huge emotional damage in the romance department with my now deceased husband. I wondered if recovery from that was harder, or easier, when the person was gone. Totally gone. There was no resolution possible because they were deceased. I could only resolve it within myself, and it had taken a long time. I was hesitant to jump back in and risk my heart again. But for Will? Yes, he might be worth the risk.

"Will." I stopped and coughed, surprised at how rough my voice sounded.

"You okay?"

"I'm fine. I was thinking about Christmas."

"A little over two weeks away."

And he spoke with a glint in his eye such that I realized with a shock that he'd surely gotten me a present.

I needed to get him one. What? I cleared my throat again.

"Yes. I was wondering if your family has traditions or such—I don't want to interfere with what your family usually does, but perhaps we could all get together for a meal during the holidays. Your mom and Britt. And you, of course."

"Do you mean here?"

Here? "Here would be fine, or at your mother's house or a restaurant. Wherever."

He nodded. "She'd love to come here."

I squeezed his arms. "Then, we'll do exactly that."

"When? Christmas Day? Or Christmas Eve?"

"Whichever." I felt a little panicky. I heard my friend Victoria's voice saying that I always looked calm and cool, but I rarely was inside. I hid it well. But this—getting to know Will's family—was something I wanted. And to do it here—at least I'd be in familiar territory. I smiled again, and this time it felt genuine. "Whichever works best for her and your family."

Will pressed a quick kiss to my lips. "She's been asking a lot of questions about you and Wildflower House." He grinned. "Just don't hold me responsible for what she asks or says." He released me and retrieved the work gloves he'd left on the counter. "Have to get going." But instead of heading to the door, he swept me into another tight hug and whispered in my ear, "Thanks for the invite, and keep the doors locked—just in case."

I pushed at his chest. "But you said not to worry?"

"Don't waste time worrying. Just flip the locks."

With that, he withdrew his arms, waved, and was gone. I followed in his wake and watched from the window as he climbed into his truck and drove off.

I agreed with him. I refused to worry. If I wanted to worry over anything, it should be about having his mother over to Christmas dinner.

And then I remembered Laura.

Well, okay. Not a big deal. In fact, we could all share a holiday meal together. Laura was family. My family should meet Will's family. It was all good. The more the merrier—or so I'd heard. I'd come to a stop in front of the foyer table with the framed photo hanging on the wall.

I'd tucked the holly sprigs I'd gathered with Laura around the frame. In the photograph, a group of women and girls were posed on my porch. They had attended school here back when the house was first built. Their white linen dresses were long, and the tips of their black button-up shoes peeked out from beneath the hems. Their hair was piled high on their heads. The younger girls wore shorter dresses but had longer curls that draped across their shoulders. The older women were garbed in black. I presumed they were teachers. Seth had found this photo among the items Sue Deale had inherited from the

Forsters. Soon after Dad and I moved in, Seth had obtained the framed photograph from Sue and had given it to us as a housewarming gift. These ladies posed on the porch— the same porch I relaxed on and welcomed my guests on— deserved to be remembered and acknowledged, and if I couldn't do that for them as individuals, then I'd acknowledge them for the women they represented.

Standing there in the wide, high-ceilinged foyer with the warmth of the wood paneling on the walls and the glossy wood floors beneath my feet, flanked by the lights and shiny glass balls of the decorated trees in the parlor and sitting room, I felt surrounded, but in a joyful way. Sue had even returned Mary's upright piano to the house, to its old accustomed space here in the foyer, and it had found renewed life here. I closed my eyes and breathed in the peace of Wildflower House.

My eyes prickled. What good fortune had brought me to this place? And what tragedy had held me here? I missed my father. Dad and I had been far from perfect, but perhaps our flaws had made us a good match despite our failures. It made our history, even the difficult parts, impossible to regret.

I slipped on my coat and took my clippers with me. I needed more holly for touches of red and green, and maybe a few fresh pine boughs, too, for their sweet, tangy evergreen aroma because Christmas was coming.

CHAPTER THREE

Wednesday, December 11 ~
Fourteen Days Until Christmas

On my first day of rest, I read, updated some files on my computer, washed laundry, and even ran the dust mop around the wood floors, but as I puttered around the huge house, my brain was busily thinking about having people over for Christmas dinner. I was more interested in planning for that than indulging in an apparently unnecessary holiday respite.

Christmas dinner. What did I envision for that? Nothing too outrageous, of course. Aunt Laura. Will's mother, Vivian, and his sister. Five altogether. I thought that sounded like a perfect grouping. Should I go with beef or turkey? Potatoes? Salad? There were lots of options.

Over breakfast the next morning, I made a shopping list with notes about gifts for Maddie, Mel, and Nicole. Victoria too. And Will. I had no idea what to get him. Not a clue. What about his mom and sister? Would they bring me a gift? Should I have something on hand in case they did?

I'd better get more tape and wrapping paper too. I checked the pantry to see what supplies I'd need for cooking and holiday baking.

In the foyer, I paused to gather my purse and keys. The beautiful trees and the other decorations—were they contributing to my mood and influencing me? Maybe. It didn't matter. I was looking forward to making this a day of checking items off my Merry Christmas list.

When Nicole called at lunchtime and asked if I'd mind having Maddie over after school tomorrow, I told her I'd be delighted.

CHAPTER FOUR

Friday, December 13 ~
Twelve Days Until Christmas

Maddie Lyn's mother died when Maddie was a toddler. At that time, Nicole, Maddie's aunt, had become her legal guardian. But Nicole had a successful career as a real estate agent, and Maddie's primary care was provided with great love by her grandmother, Mel. Mel's son, Seth, had been a huge part of Maddie's life, too, but since he'd left to take a new job in Los Angeles, the responsibility had mostly fallen on Mel, and sometimes she needed a break. Maddie and I got along well, and I was happy to fill in when needed. It was a positive arrangement for all of us.

I set Maddie's coloring books and crayons on the table in my workroom, thinking she could color or draw while I updated my business records. It was chilly and misty today, not conducive to playing outside, so later, we might watch a movie or read a book.

The storm door slammed behind her as Maddie danced in on sneakered feet. Her fine blonde hair floated around her face as I helped her shed her coat. The static charge passed from her five-year-old person to me in a quick snap. I hugged her despite the risk of further shock.

"Hey there, Maddie. Take your backpack into the workroom. We'll hang out there this afternoon."

She gave me a sweet smile. "Will we have our snack there?"

"Of course."

"Good," she said as she began to unzip her pack. "I brought dishes for us. "

Nicole, standing in the hallway, gave me a pointed look. I noted the reserve in Nicole's demeanor, and my nerves responded. Her manner was never effusive, but always professional. This was different. She motioned toward the porch and then walked away.

"Maddie, I need to speak privately with Aunt Nicole. Here are the new colored pencils." I put the box on the table next to the coloring book. "I'll be right back."

Nicole was wearing a jacket and holding a bunch of envelopes in her hand. I joined her on the porch and shivered, wishing I'd stopped to grab my own coat.

"What's wrong?" I asked.

She handed the envelopes to me. "You need to be more careful about getting in your mail."

"Ah. Well, thank you very much." She was distressed about uncollected mail? Not likely.

"Also, the reporter who did the write-up for the Louisa paper about the open house promised to send you a copy directly. It should be good advertising for Wildflower House. Let me know if you don't receive it. This time of year, people seem to lose their minds."

Like you? But I didn't say it out loud.

Nicole walked to the far end of the wraparound porch. Her arms were now tightly crossed, and her posture was rigid. "I don't want Maddie Lyn to hear. I don't want her to worry. You know how she fixates on losing her mother sometimes, even though it's been so long, and since Seth left, she's missing him too. I may be her legal guardian, but her Grammy is the steadiest, most stable influence in her life."

Mel Albers was a wiry, energetic woman of good sense and practicality. She adored her granddaughter, Maddie. And she'd been of immense help to me, especially after Dad died. We both knew what loss felt like. In fact, we *all* knew. I understood Nicole's desire to keep Maddie in the dark about any threat to her grandmother.

"What's wrong with Mel?"

"The doctor says it's her heart."

"She seemed fine at the open house."

Nicole nodded. Her expression was somber. "She had a good time at the party. But she's been . . . not quite herself recently. She has spells when she doesn't feel well."

"I noticed that. She said she'd been to the doctor and was fine. "

"She's seventy-two and generally quite fit. You know what a dynamo she can be. This is a recent decline. This morning Mom saw the specialist. I insisted on going with her. I'm glad I went. It's Mom's heart. The doctor is recommending a procedure right away to get a better look, but he's expecting she may need more, perhaps stents or even a valve replacement."

"What can I do?"

"Business-wise, this is a quiet time of year for selling houses, so I can juggle that as needed, but I must help my mother, and regardless of what the doctor does or doesn't do, there'll be some degree of worry and recovery. I want to support Mom, but I don't want Maddie subjected to all that. I don't want her worrying over maybe losing her Grammy. I'd like to keep her out of it as much as possible."

She added, "Mom is scheduled for the procedure early on Tuesday morning. The cardiac surgeon was able to fit her in, but it's very early, so she'll check into the hospital on Monday after Maddie leaves for school."

"Wow. Seems quick. I guess it's good she can be treated before the holidays?"

Nicole nodded. "I'm grateful for that. And for your help too. You'll have to drive Maddie to and from school starting Monday afternoon. The last day of school for the semester is Friday, and her Christmas pageant at the church is that evening. She has one more choir practice for the pageant on Wednesday. I'm hoping we'll be home again and back to our normal routine, or close to it, before the pageant. I wish I could tell you specifically."

"Just let me know what you need as you figure it out, and I'll handle it. What does Maddie know?"

"Just that . . ." She wrung her hands together. "I haven't told her anything because there's no need to worry her yet. She doesn't need to know until Mom is already recovering. That's soon enough. I want stability and security for Maddie. I suggested to her—and I'm sorry for using you this way—but I suggested to her that you were going to be—I'm sorry—very lonely this Christmas, and it might be nice if she could spend part of the holiday with you, even staying overnight for a few days."

"She's welcome. Now or whenever. Always. But, Nicole, you need to tell her something. Children . . ."

"Not yet. I'll tell her when and if it's necessary or appropriate."

Stress was evident in her voice. There was no value

in arguing my point at this moment.

Nicole said, "It's a little scary that the cardiologist is so intent on getting it done before the holidays. I suspect someone else got bumped from his schedule—which tells me how serious this is."

"No putting it off until after Christmas? Scary, yes. But how wonderful to start the new year with all that behind you."

"Good way to think of it. I'll try to remember." She pressed her fingers against her temples and breathed deeply, and then she said, "Maddie Lyn will stay home with us until she leaves for school on Monday, and if you could pick her up after school that day, it would be great."

"She's going to ask questions, Nicole."

"We'll deal with that as it comes up." She nodded as if she was having a separate conversation in her head and had reached a conclusion. "Mom will be fine. Of course she will. Later, we can explain that Grammy was sick but she's all better now. With a little luck, we may even have our normal Christmas."

I had my doubts, but I understood her need to protect herself—not just to protect Maddie. She was dealing with the worry in pieces—managing the blows.

"Concentrate on Mel, and on yourself too. Maddie and I will do fine. Please keep me informed, and if you need anything else at all, let me know."

"Can you bring her home at suppertime this evening? About six? We're having sandwiches and soup tonight. Keeping it simple. You can talk to Mel then, but please say nothing about her problem in front of Maddie."

"Yes, I'll be glad of the chance to see Mel before the procedure."

The relationship between Nicole and me had been contentious in the beginning. We were friends now but not exactly cozy together. I followed my impulse and hugged her. I felt her surprise in a slight moment of stiffening, of pulling away, and then the forward sag and her own arms going around me, awkwardly but there, and her face resting on my shoulder. When she stepped away, she wore a slightly sheepish expression on her face.

"Thank you, Kara. I apologize for springing this on you. I considered calling you about Maddie staying over, but I wanted to see your face when I asked. I wanted to be sure I wasn't putting you in a difficult position. Honestly, I don't know what we'd do without you."

"You'd manage. No doubt about that. But I'm grateful to be here and able to help."

Just before climbing into the car, she said, "I have a client appointment. Mom is home resting. Seth will probably come home sooner rather than later. He has to wrap up some things in LA before he leaves so that he doesn't have to rush back. Hopefully he can pick up some of the slack while he's here."

Seth. That was twice within the space of an afternoon that I'd thought of Seth. We'd been a thing at one time. Or had almost been.

I walked into the house and to the workroom.

"Maddie, I hear you're going to be visiting me next week."

"Uh-huh. For a few days. Maybe Christmas," she murmured, more focused on shading the princess's dress. "That's why I brought my dishes."

I was puzzled that she seemed so matter-of-fact, but I let it go for now.

Those tiny plastic dishes . . . The plate would hold one cookie or perhaps a single stack of cookies. The teacups could handle a swallow of drink. Maddie had arranged the place settings on the table, and they were under the supervision of a gray fuzzy bear propped against the crayon box. Maddie pushed stray staticky hairs, stuck to her cheeks, back out of the way, almost absentmindedly.

I asked, "Would you prefer chocolate chip cookies or wafers?"

"Umm." She looked up at me, considering. "Wafers."

"Got it. I'll be right back."

"Yes, ma'am." And she returned to coloring.

In the kitchen, alone, it hit me. Mel. I wished for

Will. I would've liked another hug from him. Perhaps his reassurance that Mel would be fine? Ironic that he hardly knew her though the Albers family was such a big part of life around here, and yet his reassurance would mean so much to me . . . his embrace alone had such power.

Even if Mel recovered from this, it would be something else sooner or later. Mel was in her seventies. Human bodies were mortal. Every single one. So reassurance that she'd be okay, or that no matter what happened, we'd be okay, was a treasure.

Did that sound selfish? Maybe a little. But it was also honest. And part of that honesty was the acknowledgment that parents did leave, loved ones did die, and that loving others meant that their loss or departure could irrevocably change your life. And sometimes broke your heart.

~~~~

That evening, I shared soup and grilled-cheese sandwiches with Mel, Nicole, and Maddie. All my afternoon's efforts to think of comforting, wise, or encouraging things to say vanished into nothingness as, instead, we laughed and made silly. Maddie's high-pitched giggles mingled with Mel's hoarser laughter and Nicole's admonishments about not talking or laughing or singing with food in your mouth—which she directed at Maddie, but Mel and I were guilty too. At the end of the meal, I gave Maddie a hug, and I gave Mel a longer one that ended with me pecking a quick kiss on her cheek. I stepped away, offered a smile, and then walked out with Nicole.

"You're sure?" Nicole asked.

"I am."

Nicole took my hands in hers. "Thank you, Kara. I appreciate you."

I grasped hers in return. "Same here, Nicole. Thank you. And I appreciate you too."

"Let me get you a flashlight. I wasn't thinking about how dark it would be. For that matter, why don't I drive you home?"

"I have a flashlight in my coat pocket. I'm looking forward to the walk. I love the winter air. Plus, it's quicker to walk as the crow flies than to drive around."

"You have your phone, right?"

"Of course. No worries, Nicole. I'm at home here on Cub Creek."

"You are, aren't you? There was a time when I wasn't sure you'd settle in. I'm glad you did."

I walked away, in no hurry. Despite the chill, I paused on the wooden bridge over Cub Creek.

The railing was strong after being mended a few months ago. The water rushed by below. It was the sound of continuity, of the water traveling from source to destination, only to be taken back up by evaporation and returned to its source, or a different source. It felt like a promise. An assurance. Even the life cycle of wildflowers offered proof of recurrence, of renewal.

Less than a year here, and I'd already made so many memories. Memories that would stay with me as difficult learnings or gifts of love. Whether happy memories or sad, they were within me. They ebbed and flowed much like the processes of nature.

Losses, yes. But so much had also been gained. Even so, I wasn't ready to lose anyone else. Not for a long time. As I leaned against the railing with the water flowing below and the evergreens around me offering their own special promise, I sent a prayer for Mel's well-being straight from my heart, heavenward.

CHAPTER FIVE

Saturday, December 14 ~

Eleven Days Until Christmas

I was struggling. I was worried about Mel but also about Maddie. I wanted—*I needed*—to talk to someone about it.

Mel's health problems were her private, personal information. I couldn't discuss it with anyone without her permission, and frankly, people—even well-meaning folks—would talk. Laura would've listened and offered assurance, I didn't doubt it, but she knew too many of the same people who would also know the Alberses. One careless word spoken to the wrong person—or even simply overheard—would spread. I didn't want to be the cause of Mel's personal business being out there as gossip.

Maybe Will?

It was Saturday morning. Will worked mostly Monday through Friday, but he'd been putting in extra hours to finish up the current job he was doing for Mitchell's Landscaping.

I hesitated to interrupt his work but called him anyway. "Hey, Will. You busy?"

"Was. Not now. Finished up the Slocum job first thing this morning. Now I'm over at the garage going over the equipment. I was taking my time and enjoying myself. It's peaceful out here."

"Peaceful? Sounds wonderful."

"Come over and help me clean the equipment."

"What an offer! How could I possibly turn that down, except if I recall correctly, the Mitchell Landscaping facility is over on the far side of the county. Quite a ride."

"Not so, dear Kara. I'm at the satellite location right by Cub Creek. It's a big garage with a tiny office. You haven't been over here, right? It's not far from you."

"Seriously?"

"Serious. When Jim and Libbie married, he built this garage over here for convenience."

I considered. "I don't want to interfere with your work."

"But your voice says otherwise. Besides, I could use a bite. Maybe a sandwich. It would help me out."

He was offering me an excuse. I understood he'd heard the neediness in my voice.

"I have peanut butter and jelly."

"My favorite." He gave me some quick directions,

then added, "After you pass over the concrete bridge, keep your eyes peeled for the horse farm. The place with the big garage is directly opposite. If you reach a second concrete bridge, you'll know you went too far."

I made us each a sandwich, poured some tea into glass containers with lids, and grabbed a handful of napkins, a bag of chips, and a few cookies. I dashed to the car, and to Will.

It was chilly out, but I had a warm coat and shoes. Belatedly, I thought I should've made coffee. But that would've delayed me longer, and suddenly, I was in a huge hurry.

Traveling along winding country roads could be confusing, but I found the satellite office and garage. A decorative sign down by the road read CUB CREEK, and at the top of the hill stood a beautiful white clapboard house. It looked old, but immaculate. Trim and neat. If a house could be well loved, this one was—a lot like how I felt about my own home. *My home.* The words felt right to my brain and to my heart.

The smattering of pines and oaks across the green sweep of the front yard towered over the house, making it seem both larger and smaller at the same time. The garage, on the other hand, was huge, new, and gleaming metal. It stood off to the right side at the end of the driveway. It had a large sign identifying it decisively as MITCHELL'S

LANDSCAPING—CUB CREEK FACILITY. The sign was all business, but well designed, and hung on the long wall facing the road.

As I drove up, I couldn't help but notice that the driveway was freshly paved. I wanted asphalt for my own long drive through the trees to Wildflower House. Never thought I'd be envious of a paved driveway. The idea of it amused me and made me laugh.

Will's truck was there, parked beside the house and near the garage. No one was in sight. Will had said that Jim Mitchell and his wife lived here. Maybe I was doing a little trespassing of my own? No, Will had invited me, and Will was an employee who needed lunch.

I took the bag of sandwiches and the glass jars with me. Since I was already behind the house now, it was hard not to notice the beautiful terrace and screened porch. I saw no one. The garage had multiple bays with big equipment inside. But no signs of life.

"Will?" I called out.

No Will, but a dog came running out of the woods. I stood still, frightened. I'd never owned a pet, much less a dog, and this one was big and running straight at me. He was sleek-looking and short-haired, so he wasn't a wolf or coyote, but beyond that, I couldn't tell. I held my sandwiches higher, wondering if I should toss them one way and run in the other direction . . . and then I heard

Will.

"Kara. I'm here."

"Help, Will."

Suddenly, he was there, greeting the dog and taking my bag and the jars and clearly not in the least disturbed by this unleashed animal.

"This is Max."

"Max?"

"Max. Everyone loves this guy. You will too."

"I don't know anything about dogs," I said, not quite believing him.

Will laughed, and somehow with his arms full of the lunch I'd brought, he still managed to hug and kiss me. I tried to relax. Will wouldn't be behaving this way if there was any danger.

"Come along in."

I was thinking we should get into the car to get away from the dog, who apparently wanted to meld with my legs. "We could sit in my car to eat."

"No need," Will said.

A woman strolled out of the woods. She looked about my age, maybe a couple of years older. The dog bounded back toward her as if to notify her that someone new had shown up in their territory, and he approved and was happy about it.

She smiled, pushing her long reddish-brown hair

back behind her ear and then extending her hand as she reached me. "Hi, I'm Libbie. You must be Kara. I've heard about you from my husband, Jim, and from Will, of course."

I returned her smile and held out my hand. Max lifted his muzzle and tried to lick it. Libbie intercepted him, laughed as she apologized, and shooed him off. He backed away a few feet. She took my hand and squeezed gently before releasing it.

"I've met your husband," I said.

"Yes." She looked at the bag and glass jars that Will was still holding. "Lunch?"

Will nodded.

"You're welcome to come inside to eat."

Will said, "No need. We're good. We'll eat in the office."

"It's not too chilly?"

"No, ma'am. Got a heater in there, so we're good."

She smiled again. "Then I'll let you get inside and get warmed up."

Will grinned. "We'll do that."

We turned, and as we walked into the garage, Will guided me toward the back. He said, "When you arrived, I was washing up, trying to get the top layer of grease off. Sorry I didn't hear you right away. You were quick."

It was a small office. A computer was on a table with

two chairs pulled up. A sliding window in one wall let in daylight, and a space heater was on the floor in a corner. Seeing me glance at it, Will asked, "Are you cold? I can turn it on."

Clearly, he wasn't cold. I said, "I'm fine."

We settled in the chairs and I pulled the sandwiches and a few other items from the bag. Will looked at the glass jars with their lids screwed on tightly. "Cute idea."

"It works," I said. "So that was Jim's wife? Libbie?"

"Sure. Nice lady."

"She seems . . . I don't know . . . a little shy?"

"Shy? Maybe. She's careful about getting to know people. A lot like you."

"What?" Actually, he was mostly right. "I guess I am." Not shy or standoffish by intention, but yes, I was careful. My instinct told me that Libbie Mitchell had been hurt by people she trusted, as had I. But I was learning. Learning to trust again—and to extend that trust to people who came into my life. I suspected it was the same for her.

Will waited until I'd taken a bite before he asked, "So what's on your mind?" He grinned. "I know you were probably just angling for an excuse to spend time with me . . . but I thought I heard something else in your voice too. No problems with uninvited guests?"

After a quick reflexive response, I realized he couldn't be talking about Mel and Maddie but was referring to the mystery with the candy wrapper out in the woods. "No, it's not about that. This is . . . about friends. On my mind and my heart. I don't want to gossip. I feel odd talking about other people like this."

"You trust me, right? That I won't gossip?"

"I do. Absolutely."

"Then it's up to you. You are welcome to share." He touched my cheek. "I know how it feels to have something big—big to you personally—bottled up inside."

He was referring to when Seth and I hadn't yet officially parted ways, but Will had feelings for me. I'd asked him to be patient while I figured it out with Seth, and he had been.

I rested my hand on his. "I know I can trust your discretion, but I don't want you to see me as a complainer. Even if I sometimes am."

"It's your way of figuring out the best route from point A to point B."

I liked how that sounded. Just a process. Not a flaw. I nodded.

"Then why not give it a try? Just throw it all out here, and let's see where it lands."

We heard a low whine.

"Talk about complainers," Will said.

Max was sitting outside the glass door. His nose was only a micro-distance from the door, and his earnest, hopeful eyes were trained on us.

I said, "We could let him in. Maybe he's cold?"

"He's not cold. But he does want in."

"Will the food be a problem?"

"Well, that's what he's hoping for, but it won't be a problem. He's well trained, believe it or not. And smart. He's a Weimaraner. First one I ever met. Good dog."

Max must've heard *good dog* through the closed door, because he lifted his haunches halfway off the concrete floor, and his tail wagged.

I was doubtful, but I couldn't help myself. "Okay. Let's give him a chance."

Will pushed the door open, and Max slipped in politely. "Down," Will said. And Max did, going first to a sitting position and then down to the floor. His eyes stayed on us, ever hopeful, but he stopped whining and seemed content to lie on our shoes, warming my feet nicely. It added coziness. The atmosphere, at least the piece encompassing me, seemed to relax.

"You may laugh at me—it's okay," I said. "And you are welcome to express ideas and opinions, but don't lecture or make me feel like a wretch, okay?"

"What?" He patted his pocket and checked the desktop. "Where's my pencil. I think you need to repeat all that so I can write it down."

"Oh, hush." I waved a hand at him in goodwill

annoyance. Max seemed to think the gesture was an affirmative signal to him, so I ended it quickly, and Max settled back to the floor, where he resumed watching us.

"So," I said. "The open house went well. It was great. Am I right?"

Will nodded.

"And I was thinking a quiet Christmas was exactly what I needed. It's what I'm used to."

"You don't want my mom and sister to come?"

I saw the surprise in his eyes. "No, not that at all. Absolutely I want them there." I didn't admit that I'd forgotten, that all the other worries that had come along after we discussed them coming for Christmas dinner had pushed it out of my mind. "In fact, I've also invited my aunt."

"Great. The more the merrier."

"My thought exactly. But then Nicole came over and said—" A sudden hitch in my voice stopped me. I cleared my throat and sipped my tea. I forced a smile and tried again. "She said her mother, Mel . . . " There was another sudden stop as my jaw clenched and my eyes burned.

"What about her mom? Just spit it out, Kara. Just get the words said. You'll feel better."

"She has a heart problem." My eyes filled with liquid, and something wet ran down my cheek. I brushed at it. "I'm overreacting. She'll be fine. People have heart issues fixed every day. She's lucky. Her problem was found before a terrible event happened, and she's getting medical attention, right?"

"You're thinking of your father."

I caught my lip between my teeth and held it. I bit down harder. What didn't I want to say?

"In part," I admitted. "He was so healthy. We had no idea a stroke was just lurking, waiting to happen. But mostly I'm thinking about all of them, Will. All the people I've lost and that others have lost, and now poor Maddie . . . She lost her mother when she was hardly more than a baby, and now maybe she'll . . ." I dissolved and covered my face with my hands. I felt warm pressure on my thigh as Max rested his muzzle there.

Will leaned forward and put his arms around me. He patted me on the back. The hug was a little awkward and almost made me giggle. But he meant it sincerely, and he cared. He eased his arms away and sat back in his chair. He looked me straight in the face. "You're seeing yourself in Maddie? And Maddie in you?"

I hadn't really considered it that way, but with Will saying the words, it seemed on target. I nodded.

He said, "You know what you need to do."

"I do?" He was going to tell me to deal with it. *Face it, accept it, put the worry behind you, and move on.* That had always been Dad's advice for gnarly emotional problems. Dejected, I asked, "What's that?"

"Help."

Not quite what I expected.

He said, "What do they need you to help with?"

"Nicole asked me to take care of Maddie while Mel is having the procedure and recovering."

"And you agreed."

"Of course."

Will shrugged. "Well, then, there you go. Be ready, be prepared, and be there for Maddie and Nicole too. Nicole might be grown, but this is her mom, and I'm sure she's scared."

"Face your fear by helping someone else work through theirs? Is that your point? I'm happy to help. Whatever they ask."

Help them work through their fear and vanquish your own.

A novel idea.

"You're right," I said. I had an outlet for my worry and nervous energy. Instead of having a Christmas like the ones I remembered, I was going to have—and provide—a Christmas we would never forget.

"Mrs. Albers will probably be fine, but worrying never fixed or prevented anything. Just do whatever you can to help her and the family through it."

"Feels like I should do more."

"Be available and open to what they need."

"You're pretty smart, Will Mercer."

"I'm smarter than I look, I admit that."

"Then you must be brilliant, because you look amazing."

We stood. The office was small, but we had more than enough space as he put his arms around me again. We fit well together despite the coats and work clothes. I could've stood there forever, held close in his arms and his lips near mine and our breath coming quick and light—and then Max whined, which I hardly noticed until he uttered a short, sharp bark. I pulled away. Through the window, I saw Jim Mitchell walking toward the garage. With rueful glances and flushed-face shrugs, we stepped apart.

Jim hadn't seen us, but without Max, he would've walked right in on us. And I wasn't too sure that I would've minded. I minded more that we'd been interrupted.

Still, it was Will's workplace. His job. His boss.

"Hey, Kara?"

I touched his cheek. "Yes?"

"I promised Mom to help her get Grandma's tree down from the attic this afternoon and put her outside lights up. Let's go out for lunch or supper tomorrow."

"Sounds wonderful. And you're welcome to bring

Grandma to Christmas dinner too."

He planted a quick kiss on my lips and stepped back as Jim reached the office door.

"Hey, you two." Jim extended his hand. "How're you doing, Kara?"

"Very well. It's shaping up to be a busy season."

"Christmas and holidays have a way of doing that. Just about the time I'm ready to pull my hair out, I remember that a lot of people spend it alone. Then I don't mind so much. Are you staying in town or traveling?"

"Oh, definitely here. No traveling for me."

"Getting geared up to finish the renovations? I got a look inside at the open house. It's amazing." He added, "We'll be in town too. If you need anything, just let me know."

He cast an extra, almost amused look at Will, saying, "But I'm guessing you're all set?"

Will's cheeks pinked up, and he stared at Jim.

"Merry Christmas, Kara."

"Merry Christmas, Jim."

Will walked me out.

"He's a nice man, isn't he?"

"Nice guy. Also, my boss. Gonna have to have a few words with him."

I laughed and felt delight spread through my body. The crisp December air brushed my face, and Will's arm was in mine. I couldn't imagine how this moment could possibly be any better.

"It feels good to laugh, Will. You might be annoyed with Jim, but I think I owe him—and you, of course—a big thank-you."

"Then I'm happy to be the sacrifice to his wit."

Every so often, Will uttered unexpected phrasing that rang almost like poetry. I remembered that when working on my landscaping he'd described the front acreage as having *a preponderance of pines*—saying the words casually, as if it were everyday conversation. Today it was *the sacrifice to his wit*. It was silly, but they felt like little gems, like word paintings in my brain.

I tightened my arm around his back and leaned into him, content.

Will said, "Tomorrow. Lunch. Right?"

"Or supper?"

"Lunch. There's a new place in town that I have in mind."

"It's a date."

"Excellent." He pulled work gloves from his jacket pocket. "I'd better wrap up the work here and get on to my grandparents' house."

"Go do good deeds, Will, and I'll do the same."

I drove away feeling warmed by more than the kiss. The idea of good deeds appealed to me. Because they were only good deeds if they were benefitting someone else, right? I felt light and airy. Maybe it was thanks to Will, or maybe it was the thought of the good deeds—but I was suddenly sure that everything was going to work out right.

~~~~

When I returned home, the sun was bright, and I walked out to the bench down by the creek. That wide-open holiday time I'd planned to relax in was filling up fast. No problem. I could be as flexible as I needed to be, so long as I had a chance to think it all through first.

Sitting on the bench, enjoying Cub Creek passing by and birdsong in the trees opposite, I smiled. Will's presence was here, too, as if I'd brought a piece of his heart home with me. According to him, worry was a waste. But waste or not, worry was part of the human condition and sometimes unavoidable. Will had suggested ways of turning that stumbling block of worry into positive action.

I rose. As I walked up the slope toward the house, I heard a woman's voice yelling, "There you are. Here, Kara!"

Victoria. She'd helped me with the open house and then driven back home to Richmond. What was she doing here again so soon? Given that I'd barely hit that *I'm okay, and I've got a handle on things* state, I felt a stab of alarm as she rushed across the yard to reach me. She was wearing jeans. Unusual for her. Yoga or tailored-looking stretch pants were more her style. Before she could explain, I was already assuming she'd lost her job—the one she'd just started after losing the prior one.

"Kara, Kara, Kara. I'm so excited, and you will be too." She grabbed my arm and propelled me alongside her up the slope to the house.

"Good grief, Victoria. What's up with you?" But I laughed as I said it. Victoria was, indeed, the force of nature that she claimed to be. Enthusiastic about almost everything. Sometimes that took her too far, beyond good sense.

"Not *good grief*, but *good news*. Excellent news. Mom, my aunt, and my brother are spending Christmas with family in Michigan. I can't go because of my job. I'm too new to get that kind of vacation time."

She didn't sound disappointed to miss out on the trip, but rather relieved.

"I'm glad for your mother, but I don't quite understand the good news. You aren't *that* eager to get rid of them, are you?" I was teasing, but only a little.

"No, silly, that's not the good news. Just listen." She put her hands up to emphasize the listening part. "I can't get off from work for the holidays, but I also can't go into the office because the building is old and needs work.

Most of us are being told to work from home. Remotely. Until the first week of January." She practically danced in excitement. "Isn't that great?"

By now we'd reached the terrace. We paused at the foot of the steps leading up to the back porch.

"I don't understand how that's great, or even good news."

"Because," she said, facing me and spreading her arms wide to shout the news, "it means I can spend Christmas with you here at Wildflower House!"

She leaned toward me, and in a slightly lowered voice, as if we weren't alone in the middle of many acres of land, she said, "I was so worried about you being alone this Christmas. I thought I'd just be coming up for a day during the holidays. But this is perfect. I can work from here. We can hang out for the whole week. Maybe roast marshmallows over a fire or do more decorating or whatever. We can make this Christmas rejuvenating and extra special. And you won't be alone."

Good news? Good grief. She was so excited, meant so well, all good stuff.

Maybe the doubts that were swirling in my head were also showing on my face because Victoria's arms came down to her sides, and the animation left her face.

"Am I intruding? I don't want to push in. I'm sorry, I should've phrased it differently. Asked instead of proclaiming." She forced a small smile. "I should've called first."

She was backing away emotionally and even physically. I grabbed her arms this time.

"No. Wait. I have things to tell you."

"If it's Will, I understand. I don't want to be a third wheel. Been there, done that, right?"

"Nothing like that, Victoria." I added, "This is about someone else. Let's go inside and have a cup of coffee or maybe some tea. Let's take a moment to talk."

I wanted to laugh at myself and at her plan to save me from spending Christmas alone, but the look of hurt and confusion on her face silenced me.

"Victoria," I said, "when you hear what's going on around here, you may change your mind about where you'll find a peaceful, rejuvenating holiday, and where you'd like to spend Christmas."

"What do you mean?"

"This is private. It's someone else's personal information. If I tell you, you must promise not to talk to anyone else about it—other than me—even if you mean well . . ."

"Of course. Who? What?"

I led her up the steps to the back door and insisted we sit at the kitchen table.

"Mel is having heart problems. She's checking into

the hospital on Monday for a procedure to check out her heart. I don't know exactly—I don't think they know precisely either yet—but it sounds like they'll need to insert stents, or possibly more, as I understand it. It's scheduled for early Tuesday. I don't know exactly how long the recovery will be, but starting Monday afternoon, Maddie will be staying here with me. Maddie doesn't know anything, or if she does somehow, she doesn't know how serious it is. Nicole has asked me not to tell her about Mel's condition."

"She'll be fine, I'm sure, and I'll keep my mouth shut about it. And I can help," Victoria said. "Maddie and I are buddies." She leaned closer. "Face it, Kara—neither of us is used to having kids around 24-7, so I'll be even more helpful than I knew."

She was making sense.

"Do you have a room fixed up for her?"

"She'll stay in the room next to mine. There are twin beds in there now."

"Yep, I noticed that when I was here for the open house and did a little snooping. Hey, twin beds are a good idea. You'll be able to offer guests a variety of sleeping arrangements. But what I'm asking is, did you decorate it?"

"What do you mean?"

She shrugged. "She's a little kid. She's never stayed

here overnight before, has she? It should feel homey, friendly. Welcoming."

"No. And no, I don't have anything on the walls or such, if that's what you mean."

"I have an idea. I have things left over from my own misspent childhood—back when I thought I wanted to be a princess too. Mom kept everything. I'll bring it all back with me tomorrow, and we'll get the room fixed up for her."

"I don't want to overdo."

"We'll make her comfy." She slapped her hands against the kitchen table like a trumpet flourish. "It's settled, then. What time do you expect her on Monday?"

"After school."

"Then we'll get this done tomorrow. Unfortunately, I can't stay today, plus I need to go home for everything, including my work computer, before I can settle in here. Luckily, you've got good internet, or this wouldn't work for me. I suppose I could use my phone for a hotspot, if necessary."

Settle in here?

She continued, "So let's go upstairs and see what we have to work with. Do you still have boxes stacked in that room?"

"A few. Only three or so."

"We need to clear those out." She was already

walking up the stairs. "I'm sorry I can't stay today. But I'll be back tomorrow afternoon, and we'll get the facelift done with time to spare."

She didn't wait for a response.

Astonished . . . that's what I was, though I shouldn't have been.

I followed Victoria and joined her in the guest room to discuss how to prepare a proper princess room for Maddie.

Astonished? Yes, I was. But perhaps I was astonished that I hadn't thought to do it on my own and grateful that Victoria had.

~~~~

Victoria left declaring that she'd be back tomorrow afternoon with the princess goods. I felt like I'd been buffeted by a whirlwind. But by a smart whirlwind with good instincts.

I wished I'd thought of tweaking the guest room to make it more interesting to a little girl. I told myself that I would've thought of it on my own, given time and space, but probably not. Because we knew what we knew, right? The rest of it we had to learn. Or not.

That evening, standing on the back porch in my robe, and with the sofa blanket wrapped around me for extra warmth, I watched the night. My breath was frosty. I wouldn't stay out long. I'd had an overwhelming need to see the view—the stars, the garden, and the creek in the distance picking up whatever reflected light that happened to fall upon it.

Mel. From the first time I'd met her, right here at Wildflower House, I'd been drawn to her. As the strong mother figure I'd never had? Or the loving but wise grandmother I'd wished for when I was a kid? Or simply as a friend? Sometimes the best friends are the ones with whom you have things in common but not a messy personal history. There was value in those baggage-free relationships that had no history to bind or to separate as there was with Victoria and me.

I sighed, and a thin wisp of breath materialized in front of me. It dispersed as it cooled in the winter night. Everything moved on. Good and bad.

Good deeds. Be there to help.

I liked that.

CHAPTER SIX

Sunday, December 15 ~
Ten Days Until Christmas

On Sunday afternoon, Will arrived on my doorstep at precisely 12:30 p.m. He was carrying a potted plant.

I was expecting him, of course, but surprised to see him holding the plant.

"For me?"

"Well, I considered keeping it as a sidekick. You know, just me and my Christmas cactus cruising around Louisa County together. Hanging out." He touched the long fronds that arched out of the pot. "Get it? Hanging out?"

He handed the plant to me. The green branches with their succulent leaves had lots of tight, tiny red buds, chock-full of potential blooms.

"I do get it." I shook my head and shrugged. "Mildly amusing."

He frowned. "Tough crowd."

"Not so tough. In fact, getting more softhearted by the minute. I'm glad to see you. Would you like to come in?"

"That's the plan, right?"

I carried the plant to the kitchen. "The plan? As in going out to lunch?"

Will said, "It needs water. And yes, that's the plan, unless you'd like to hang here instead?" He'd stopped near me, very near.

"Stay here?" I echoed. "I suppose we could."

"It's a nice place. Good ambience."

"Are you looking for ambience?"

"Not necessarily."

It seemed inevitable that I would turn toward him and that he would move even closer.

I whispered, "Thank you for my plant."

He said, his breath warm against my ear, "I wanted to bring you fresh-cut flowers . . . but it's winter, and the grocery store was out of stock. I saw the cactus and thought of you."

Was he saying that I could be prickly? "Thank you? I think?"

"I saw the cactus and all of those buds, and I thought of you and flowers and spring, and butterflies and honeybees and lots of good things ahead of us."

I touched his cheek. "Very romantic."

Will nodded. Our arms moved in unison, finding their way around each other, even as our lips met. I don't know how long we stood there in that embrace—only that it ended when the doorbell rang.

He pulled back. "What are our options?"

Laughing, I stood on tiptoe and kissed him again and then went to answer the door. No one ever rang the doorbell. In fact, I saw the front door was almost fully closed. I was sure I'd left it open, trusting the storm door to keep out most of the winter chill. I paused, shrugged, and opened it wide.

Laura was standing there. Her face was bright red. As if she might've been in a footrace or fresh from a sauna . . . or perhaps had just caught her niece in a passionate embrace with a handsome man in the kitchen. Laura knew Will, of course, but that probably hadn't done anything to lessen her embarrassment.

I opened the storm door. "Come in."

Laura stammered, "Just dropped by . . . I dropped by to drop this off . . . to . . ." She was holding a covered dish.

"It's okay, Aunt Laura. You are welcome."

"I should've knocked before walking in. I should've just left and not . . ."

"I'm glad you stayed. Come in and say hello to Will."

"Are you sure? I'm so sorry."

"It's okay. Will and I have kissed before, and I'm quite sure we will again."

By then we were standing in the foyer. Will walked in and gave Laura a huge grin. She started giggling and put a hand over her face. She shook her head. "You two," she said. "What a pair you are! You make a lovely couple." She handed me the dish she'd been holding. "I brought you bread pudding. I hope you'll like it."

Will grinned again. "I love it. Would you care to join us? We're dining in today."

"Oh, no, goodness. I can't. I have to get on home."

"Why not join us?" I asked. Taking Will's cue, I was about to say I could rustle up a meal in no time, when Will interrupted.

"I have steaks. Steaks and baked potatoes. Forgot the bags out in the car."

"In the car," I echoed, giving him a sharp look.

"Plenty of food," he said. "Would you join us?"

"I'd be delighted to, if you're sure."

"Certain sure," he said. "I'll go grab those groceries. Be right back."

As Will went outside, Laura came close to me and whispered, "You should be more careful about that door, sweetheart. You never can tell who might come waltzing in or what they might be interrupting."

"Yes, ma'am, I'll keep that in mind."

Will brought the groceries in—steaks and more. "I'll do the cooking, if you're okay with that."

"Fine with me. I'll set the table."

Laura helped, and as we arranged the napkins and flatware next to the plates, she said, "I did drop by for more than the bread pudding. I wanted to talk to you about something."

"What?"

"It'll be quick."

"Will? You okay here? Laura and I are going to step into the sitting room."

"I'm good. You've got some time."

"Let's go, then."

We went to the sitting room, where my chair and Dad's chair awaited. Our arrangement of years, regardless of house or address. Laura and I sat, but she balanced on the edge of her seat, so I did the same. Our knees were almost touching.

Her voice was soft as usual, with gentleness in every syllable. She clasped her hands together. "I need to apologize and also to thank you."

"For what? I hope this isn't about when you came in and Will and I—"

"No, dear. This is about my brother Lewis."

I started to speak, and she held up a hand indicating silence. "You expressed such certainty that we would find him. I tried to be as positive so I could sound certain too. But I doubted. From the time we first discussed this back in October to just the other day, I didn't believe it would ever work out."

Doubts were natural. I wanted to tell her that, but again she silenced me with one raised hand.

"Yesterday I awoke with the certainty that you are right. We will find him. Even after almost fifty years. I no longer doubt. I've had my disappointments in life. I've also had many blessings. Doubt never fixed a problem or solved any challenge." She nodded, as if checking to be sure she'd gotten her speech said as planned.

She continued, "So I wanted to come here today. In fact, just this morning the pastor preached about belief and faith and that it's okay to hope and to pray for things that . . . matter to you. I had to tell you about my doubt and that I now believe in this quest to find Lewis. I believe in my heart that if we continue trying, we will succeed. I wanted to thank you."

I was silent. She looked at me curiously. "You may speak now."

But I couldn't. I was speechless.

She reached across and put her hand on my knee. "We will find him."

Oh no. My eyes were about to leak. I felt the telltale stinging of salty tears wanting to erupt. But not really tears of joy. Almost of guilt. What had I done? I'd meant well, but I hadn't intended to get her hopes up so very high that . . . I couldn't even think of it. The disappointment of failure. Of letting her down when she believed in me.

"Laura. Dear Aunt Laura. I can't promise. If I made you believe . . . if I gave you false hope, I'm sorry. I'll try. We'll try. But I can't promise success. I can't make a miracle happen."

"Hush. It's okay. I know you can't. But I know He can." She pointed up, then pressed her hand to her heart. "If Lewis is supposed to return to us, he will. We just have to do our part. We must hope and pray, and if we can think of positive actions to take, we'll be ready to do those too."

She stood abruptly, took my hands, and tugged me up from the chair. My legs felt weak. She patted my cheek.

"Pull yourself together now," Aunt Laura said. "I don't recall the last time a man ever cooked for me, and it smells like you've got one who *can* cook." She smiled, and her eyes looked brighter than they had since I'd met her.

"Then let's eat." I put my arm through hers, and we rejoined Will in the kitchen.

CHAPTER SEVEN

Later that afternoon, Victoria arrived. I heard the squeal of her car brakes and the gravel crunching in the driveway.

She always relied too much on the last-minute application of brakes to prevent disaster. Thus far it had worked for her, but in the larger things of life—the actions that impacted others—it didn't always work in time to prevent an ill-considered act. It said a lot about her personality. Impulsive, often self-focused or self-serving, but usually lucky. It was that same trait, sometimes a flaw, that empowered her to make grand, loving gestures like bringing her childhood treasures to decorate a room for a little girl she didn't know all that well and whose stay would be temporary. If she'd really wanted to get rid of the bedspread and curtains and such, she could easily have dropped it all off at a thrift shop or dumped it into a trash bin and been done with it.

Will and Laura had left a short time ago. He'd offered to stay and move the boxes from the guest room to the attic, and even to help decorate, but I'd let him off the hook. He shouldn't suffer for being a nice guy. Will, surrounded by princess decor . . . I couldn't help chuckling at that image. I'd given him a kiss and a hug and had sent him on his way.

This had shaped up to be quite a day already, and it wasn't done yet.

By the time I reached the front door, Victoria had already opened the car trunk. I pushed the storm door wide and leaned out. "Need help?"

"Yes, please."

Her voice sounded muffled. When she stepped back, I saw why. Her arms were full of pink and purple fabric. Bedspread? Pillows? Hard to make out exactly what was in the jumble that was overflowing the box she was holding.

"Can you grab some of this stuff?" She nodded toward the trunk as she moved to the porch. She dropped the box on the steps.

"Sure."

Yes, more stuff. A child's fairy-tale lamp. A picture of a princess in a shell-covered frame. Frilly curtains.

"Curtains? Really?"

Victoria laughed and spread her arms wide in a big shrug. "They were stored with all the rest of this stuff, so I brought them along. We'll use them or not. One thing is certain—they aren't going back to Mom's house. This is my excuse for finding them a new home—a little girl who needs them."

I moved closer to her. "This is temporary."

"Get rid of it however you want after Maddie goes home. At least I'll have a few less things to go through and ditch after Mom passes."

"Harsh."

"Really? Don't judge me. You haven't seen her attic." She laughed again and shoved the edges of a pink quilted bedspread back into the box. "I'll meet you upstairs. Can you close the trunk? Thanks." And she was gone inside.

I took the lightweight cotton curtains that were falling over the side of the box. I tried to fold them, but they resisted. How did people fold ruffles anyway? I never had. *Hah.* I'd never had ruffles to fold. I dropped them into the box on top of the lamp and whatever else was in there and carried it up to the house.

Victoria and I were about to have a decorating party.

~~~

"Victoria, can I get you something to drink? A soda or tea or what?"

"Let's get this stuff laid out, and then we can have a drink while we're deciding."

Deciding what? I didn't ask, because I already knew. "How difficult can the decorating be, really?"

She stared at me, one eyebrow quirked up in a slight exaggeration. Her hand, poised on her hip, clutched a fistful of bedsheet printed with faded strawberries. "Is there some kind of rush I don't know about? You have plans tonight?"

"No."

"You never had a princess bedroom, did you?" Her eyebrow had resumed its normal position, and now she was holding on to the sheet with both hands, waiting for me to answer.

"Oh, come on, Vic. Not every child has a fairy-tale bedroom. Just because you did . . ."

"Enough, Kara. You're going to have one now, albeit vicariously through Maddie Lyn. So have fun and just roll with it."

I nodded. There were a couple of boxes in the corner that had never been moved up to the attic. "I'll get those out of the way."

"Need help?"

"No, I can handle it, and then I'll fetch us something to drink."

I carried the boxes one by one to the base of the attic stairs, then turned on the stairway light and took them the rest of the way up.

~~~~

On this December afternoon, the attic was shadowy. Daylight came in through the windows, but most was blocked by the partitioned areas. Those areas were dark and felt a little creepy, but the large open area at the front of the house near the turret had good windows and warm light. It lured me forward. The sky outside was touched with shades of lilac and pink as the sunset reached around from where the sun was setting behind the house. Everything inside and out was washed in soft, faded pastel shades.

An old chair had been left near the turret windows. I sat on the edge. I couldn't stay because I had to do my part in fixing up the room for Maddie. And I wanted to. Victoria was right. I should embrace the chance for a little fun.

Would Maddie care? Surely not. In fact, she might think I was trying to turn this visit into a more permanent arrangement. Would that frighten her? Because at some point, she was going to understand that her beloved Grammy and primary caretaker was very sick.

Nicole said Maddie didn't remember her mother, but Maddie had told me she did. My aunt had been very young when she was adopted. She claimed to remember little except for snippets of her twin and maybe of an older boy named Henry. But then, Laura had had a lot of time to forget. Or maybe it was just that memories functioned differently depending on the person or circumstance.

Did it matter? Not really. All of us had to work with what we had. With what our memories had kept available for us.

No, I hadn't had a princess bedroom. Had never given it a thought.

Well, one thing was true—Sue had said I was lucky to already have the Christmas decorating done. I was especially glad for Maddie, because if left to me, this holiday time of year would be rather drab around here. Not by choice, but simply because it was what I was used to.

"Kara? You still up there?"

I stood. "I am. Coming down now."

But Victoria was already up. She joined me.

"Cool place."

"Cold."

"Not heated."

"And hot in the summer."

"But it's a neat place. Maybe someday."

"No *maybe someday*s. I've got enough to handle as it is." I shook my head and sighed. "Believe it or not, I thought I was going to have a quiet Christmas."

"Is that what you wanted?"

I shrugged. "Thought so. At first."

Victoria tilted her head, and I anticipated another question, but instead she said, "And then you got lucky."

"That's me," I said with a wry twist. "One lucky girl."

Her face went briefly blank, and then she shook her head slowly. She put her hand on mine. "You are. Trust me, Kara. Not everything has been easy for you, but you're still standing and flourishing. Don't overthink it. Just ditch some of the baggage and enjoy the ride."

In my mind, I saw Maddie's sweet face. If she was aware of the threat to her known world, and small adjustments could make her feel cozier, then our effort was worth it.

"Well said, Victoria. I'll get us some tea, and we'll do this job right."

CHAPTER EIGHT

Monday, December 16 ~
Nine Days Until Christmas

Nicole retrieved Maddie's suitcase from the car. As she handed the case to me, we shared a look that acknowledged things didn't always work out, but that the belief they would was essential. In that one swift glance, I understood that I could be part of the belief club, right along with Nicole.

I smiled despite the worry. Yesterday I'd been inducted into the princess club by Victoria. Frivolous? Probably. Vital? Almost certainly.

Maddie and I waved goodbye to Nicole as she drove off, and then Maddie inched her hand into mine.

In a stuffy, formal tone, I said, "Miss Maddie Lyn, we have a special room prepared for you. Not the presidential suite, but we do have princess accommodations that we hope you will find suitable."

She looked puzzled. She'd been upstairs many

times, of course.

Dropping the pretense of formality, I asked, "Want to see?"

She nodded eagerly.

"Let's go, then."

As we climbed the stairs, Victoria joined us. She'd been in her room working at her computer.

"Hey, Maddie!"

Victoria was excited, but I gave her credit that she stood back and didn't rush with Maddie into the bedroom.

Maddie stood in the open doorway. "Oh," she said in a way that spoke of dreams and hopes.

In fact, standing there behind her, I wasn't seeing the faded bedspread and tired flounces, nor the dated styles of cast-off furnishings and left-behind dreams. But items shiny and full of life yet. A room fit for five-year-old royalty.

Wildflower House was filled with antiques and mementos from the past. Why not these too?

~~~~

Maddie giggled with Victoria while we cooked an early supper. She helped set the table. She never complained, and even ate all her vegetables. By then, I was suspicious.

In between laughing with us, Maddie was very

quiet. She was agreeable, but then she was almost always agreeable. However, *quiet* was not her normal state. I'd noticed as the afternoon wore into evening and Nicole didn't return, Maddie grew more and more silent.

This time of year, the days were short, but there was still light left, so I invited Maddie to take a walk with me. Feeling that warm, small, trusting hand in mine as we strolled down toward the creek, I wondered what she was thinking. Children were perceptive. She had to know her beloved Grammy had a problem. She must've picked up on Nicole's distress. And yet she said nothing.

We were so near the creek path. The path continued to our right beyond my yard to the wooden bridge to her Grammy's house. How many times had Maddie and I followed that path? She knew the way back to her normal life, yet she wasn't suggesting we go visit Grammy, so she must know something was up. Maddie was aware of much more than her aunt wanted to acknowledge.

I squeezed Maddie's hand gently. "Let's rest on the bench for a minute, Maddie Lyn."

"Yes, ma'am." She sat beside me and scooted back. Her legs dangled, and she swung them in a natural sort of way.

She gave every appearance of docile relaxation.

Again, not our Maddie.

"What's wrong, sweetie?" I asked, my hand on her

small shoulder.

She glanced up at me, then away again quickly.

"Are you homesick?"

"No, ma'am."

"Shall I keep guessing?"

She went silent.

"So," I said. "I'm glad you came to visit. Do you like the room? Victoria and I decorated it especially for you."

"Yup."

Try again, Kara.

"What did Aunt Nicole tell you about the visit?"

"That I could visit you for Christmas."

"Because I might be lonely?"

"Uh-huh."

"I appreciate that. It's very thoughtful." I rubbed her shoulder ever so gently. "Are you okay with being here?"

She nodded.

"But you're worried about something?"

She drew in a swift breath. I felt her inner struggle.

"You can talk to me, you know that. We're friends."

She started to speak, then looked down at her hands, and in a measured voice she said, "If I stay . . . how will Santa know where to find me?"

There was a barely perceptible quaver in her voice. So it wasn't about Mel. She was worried about Santa.

Maybe Nicole was right. I felt relief.

"Not a problem. Santa keeps track of all that kind of stuff. He'll know where to find you, whether you're here or back home with Nicole and Grammy."

"Are you sure?"

"I'm very sure. I know it for certain sure."

She released a long, heartfelt sigh.

"Anything else on your mind? You're awfully quiet. Not at all like my Maddie Lyn."

She entwined her fingers. "Grammy's sick."

"She is?" Nicole was wrong. *Doggone it. Now what?*

"I have to be quiet so I won't make her tired, and then I can go back home."

Someone had said something. I presumed Nicole, but Maddie could've overheard anything—possibly even Nicole on the phone explaining to Seth about Mel's condition and Maddie coming to visit me—and had totally misinterpreted. Nicole wasn't maternal, but she loved her niece and would never have said such a thing to Maddie.

"I think you misunderstood." I brushed my hand across her long blonde curls. "Grammy might be sick, but the doctor is going to make her better. It might take a little while. But it has nothing to do with you or how much you talk or play. Grammy loves to listen to you talk and sing."

A tiny nod. "She does."

"Your Aunt Nicole might have been worried that Grammy wouldn't rest properly because she'd rather be playing with you, so while the doctor is fixing her, you are staying with me. It isn't because she doesn't want you around."

She looked up and fixed her blue eyes on mine. "Think so?"

"I know so."

After a long silent moment during which the creek, only a few yards from our feet, gurgled along and a lone bird called from somewhere nearby, Maddie came alive. She hiked up the sleeves of her sweater. "Maybe I can draw pictures for Grammy, so she can see me but not get tired?"

"I think that's a splendid idea."

She repeated softly, "Splendid." She took my hand. "It's a happy word, isn't it, Aunt Kara?"

"It is a delightfully happy word, sweetheart." Her words resonated warmly in my heart, mostly because somewhere over the recent weeks I'd gone from being *Miss Kara* to *Aunt Kara*. I'd become part of the family— at least in Maddie's world.

~~~~

I ran a bath in the old claw-foot tub in the bathroom next

to my bedroom. Maddie had always been fascinated by it. I added extra bubbles. I left her alone for privacy but with the door cracked and me within earshot. I insisted on rinsing her hair myself to get all the suds out of it, and she allowed me to help her out of the tub and dry her hair.

After she was tucked in, I sat beside her on the bed and read the book she'd brought. I sensed worry but also peace from her. I understood that Maddie felt the same as I did here in this big old house full of shadows and drafts, but also of warmth and light. We felt safe here.

Her furry bear was in the crook of one arm, and a cloth doll was in the crook of the other.

"Are you comfortable? Warm enough?"

"Yes, ma'am."

"I'm going to leave your door open and mine, too, so you can call me or come find me if you need to. But don't go near the stairs, okay? They are steep. They can be tricky in the dark. I put a cup beside the bathroom sink, so if you are thirsty, it's there for you." I smoothed her coverlet. "Remember, Victoria is just down the hall, too, so you are surrounded by people who love you."

CHAPTER NINE

Tuesday, December 17 ~

Eight Days Until Christmas

The next day, after dropping Maddie off at school, I returned home to find Victoria on her computer and wearing a headset. A meeting. She'd warned me beforehand. I didn't want to distract her, so I stepped softly down the hall. A short time later, she found me in the sitting room and asked, "Are you looking for me, Kara?"

"Sorry. I hope I didn't disturb you."

"Nope. It's all good. Any word on Mel?"

I shook my head. "Not yet."

"The morning's half gone."

"Soon. I'm sure Nicole will call us anytime now."

"You doing okay? Nerves-wise?"

"Sure. And I've got a favor to ask of you—a mission, should you choose to accept it," I added playfully, trying to lighten our worry.

"What's that?"

"Santa. We need to make sure he knows where Maddie is. Just in case she's still here Christmas morning."

"Happy to. Shouldn't we check with Nicole about what she has planned?"

I sighed. "I don't want to distract her right now. We still have a week before Christmas, so we've got time, thank goodness, but I need your help to make sure everything is ready for Santa, including stockings. We'll be prepared, even if it means we are ultimately overprepared. I don't want to be responsible for a disappointment of such magnitude, not if I can help it."

Victoria gave me a crooked grin. She shook her head. "Heaven forbid."

"Don't patronize. You are the girl with the princess bedroom—who kept her stuff all these years."

"Mom did."

"Sure, blame your mother." I walked away before she could see me smiling.

"Seriously, it was Mom."

"Uh-huh." I tried not to show the laughter I was holding in.

Victoria went silent for a long moment. "You're teasing me."

I shrugged.

She said, "You have a sense of humor? Where'd you

find it? It's been packed away for a long time."

I heard no reciprocal teasing in her voice. I turned to face her, and she apologized. "I meant it as a joke. I thought we were joking. Don't look so serious. You haven't had a lot to laugh about in the last few years." She frowned. "Or maybe you have, and I was just too thickheaded to get the joke?"

"No, you're right. Dad didn't . . . well, he didn't really get jokes. It wasn't something we indulged in."

"Well, that needs to change, because Maddie is barely five, and her whole world is full of magic and laughter and dancing. Let's join her and use her as our excuse to feel that free again."

I laughed a little, feeling all shivery and shrugging to hide it. "We'll do that for Maddie."

"Yes, ma'am. It's our duty."

"Our duty?" I nodded. "Yes, we can do this. And if we overdo the presents? We'll make some lovely donations elsewhere. How does that sound?"

"Perfect. I have another short meeting to dial into, and then I'll take off. Amazing how the morning is flying. If she gets home before I do and asks where I am, tell her I'm on a secret mission."

I frowned. "A secret mission? Won't that give it away?"

"Are you freaking kidding me? Not at all. Anyone

who doesn't have a secret mission or two underway during the holidays isn't really living."

"Okay, then."

"Stockings . . . stuffers . . . some nicer stuff. Do you have lots of wrapping paper?" Victoria asked.

"I do. But I may need more."

"I'll bet you have all that pretty red and gold foil paper."

"Well, blue and green, but yes, it's foil."

Victoria made a rude noise. "We need Santa and snowmen paper. I'll handle it."

"Hold on a minute." I found my wallet and took out a card. I handed it to her. "This is on me. My tab."

"Seriously?"

"Go for it. I mean it."

"I'll be back." As she walked away, she called back, "At least as soon as my trip to Europe is done. I hope you've got a high limit on this bit of plastic . . ."

When had I learned to trust her again? We each had to look past the other's flaws to see the value there. I didn't know if it would last, but I hoped so.

Plus, this responsibility and all that it involved was on me. Maddie was a responsibility I was happy to take on, and I could afford this. Victoria had the ideas and the energy, and a certain generosity of spirit along with questionable judgement that sometimes got her into trouble. Between us, we made a good team and could keep Maddie happily distracted.

In a change of tone, Victoria added, "Let me know if you hear anything about Mel."

As if on cue, my phone rang. We both stared at it.

Victoria said, "Answer it, Kara."

CHAPTER TEN

I grabbed the phone.

Nicole said, "Mom came through the procedure well."

My knees felt weak. I sat in my chair. "What did the doctor say?"

"The doctor was very pleased. The stents went in fine. The valve is good for now. They'll keep a watch on it. He said she'll be ready to go home in a couple of days. Hard to imagine that, but I'm thrilled."

"Are you okay, Nicole?"

"I'm good. It felt like it took forever, but I'm so grateful they were able to get her in so quickly."

"Did Seth's flight arrive in time?"

"He arrived late yesterday, but in time to visit with her. I don't think he'll be here long."

"At least through Christmas?"

"I don't know what he'll do." Nicole sounded tense.

"You don't sound like yourself."

"I'm fine. It's just . . . you know how a person gets

shaky when the worst is past? The adrenaline goes down, and suddenly you feel it. But it's all good now."

"If you need me, let me know. Victoria is here, and she and Maddie are very comfortable together, so I can come over."

"Thanks, but we're good, at least until Mom starts feeling better and tries to do too much too soon. I can see that happening in the near future."

"We'll deal with that when the time comes. Gladly." Mel had come through the procedure well. Now it was just a matter of getting her home and herself again.

"Is Maddie okay?"

"She's good." I paused. "You should know I've had to tell her some things about Mel and the procedure. Nothing specific about the ailment and the treatment."

"I trust you, Kara. I was foolish to think she didn't know something was going on. I'm glad, really, that you've talked to her about it. She has choir practice tomorrow evening. Even if Mom is back home, I think you'll need to take her.

"Of course. It's already on my calendar. No worries, Nicole. Focus on your mom and yourself."

~~~~

That afternoon, after picking up Maddie and getting her

back to Wildflower House, I sat with her at the kitchen table and explained that her grandmother had had to go to the doctor at the hospital, but that he'd fixed her heart this morning and now she had to wait a couple of days before coming home.

"When she does come home, Grammy will need to rest for a few days. I hope you won't mind staying here with me for a little longer?"

"She's okay?"

"She's good. Doing very well. Nicole will call later today, and you can speak with them both on the phone."

"Promise?"

"I promise." I felt uneasy. I seemed to be promising a lot these days. And this was yet one more promise I truly had no ability to fulfill because the results depended on others.

But Maddie was barely five. What else was I supposed to do?

"Only three more days of school before the Christmas holiday break. Ready for some time off?"

She gave me a blank look.

How silly of me. Maddie loved school. She loved being around the other children, and she loved learning. I gave her a hug and a swift peck on the forehead.

"Finish your snack, Maddie, and we'll find something fun to do."

Chapter Eleven

Thursday, December 19 ~
Six days before Christmas

Maddie's final choir practice for the pageant had been held the evening before and today was her next-to-the last day of school before the holidays. This was an important day for Mel, too, having been released from the hospital in the morning and home by lunchtime. Nicole called a little past noon and asked me to bring Maddie over for a short visit after school. In fact, Grammy was insisting on seeing Maddie before she would agree to take a nap.

I picked Maddie up a little early and we went straight home. Maddie dropped her bookbag in the hallway, grabbed the new drawings she'd done for Grammy, and we headed over. When we arrived on Mel's porch, the door was answered by Nicole and a woman I didn't know.

Nicole explained, "I've hired someone to help us out." Then she turned to Maddie and knelt to give her a big hug. "How are you doing, my sweetest girl? I've missed you. Grammy has too. We aren't the same without you."

Maddie's eyes were big, glued on her grandmother's face. Fatigue was obvious in Mel's posture, and the lines in her face looked deeper. I knew Maddie must be seeing that too. Mel extended her hand to Maddie, who moved closer and took it in her own, ever so gently.

I was glad for this chance to visit Mel, but where was Seth? Why wasn't he here to hug and fuss over Maddie Lyn? I shot a look at Nicole.

Mel was reassuring Maddie. "I'm good, baby girl. Better every minute. Thank you for my beautiful drawings. I kept them with me the whole time. The doctor said they were the best medicine of all."

Maddie's uncertainty changed to a bright smile. She offered the new drawings she was holding. Mel took them and exclaimed over their perfection. Maddie glowed. As they chatted, Nicole pulled me into the kitchen.

"Where's Seth?" I asked.

"He had to make an emergency run for some things for Mom. He thought he'd be back quicker but ran into some problems."

"Maddie hasn't mentioned him at all. At all. Which tells me he is very much on her mind. You know how she does." I crossed my arms. "Tell me honestly, Nicole. Is he avoiding me? Am I the problem?"

"I don't think so. He's been focused on Mom. He wants to spend time with Maddie when it's calmer and not so rushed."

We both heard Mel's voice as she asked, "Do you mind staying with Aunt Kara a little while longer? I think you'll have more fun since I need to rest a lot for a few more days."

Maddie asked, "Will you come to the Christmas pageant?"

"I will. At least, I will do my best to be there. Do you understand?"

Maddie nodded. "Okay, but I want to see you every day." She said it again, emphasizing those words. "Every. Day."

"It's a deal, sugar. You are, and always will be, my best medicine."

I said to Nicole, "Tell him to come see her. To drop by the house anytime. He's always welcome."

CHAPTER TWELVE

Will joined us for supper that evening. I was especially grateful, because Maddie had grown increasingly subdued as we'd walked home from Mel's house. She sat quietly, cocooned in her thoughts, while Victoria cooked the chopped steak and gravy and I mixed the salad.

I called out, "Maddie, set the table, please."

She responded, setting out the dishes and flatware, but with no energy or engagement.

Will arrived with a coconut cream pie.

"From Mom."

"Wow. Please thank her." I accepted the dish from him.

"You'll get to do that yourself in a few days."

I felt a little anxiety about meeting his mom, especially with other Christmas dinner guests standing around, but I didn't want Will to interpret my worry as regret over having made the invitation, so I said quickly, "I'll do that, and gladly."

After supper, I was in the kitchen doing a last tidy-up when I heard the plinking of piano keys and thought of Maddie, and then the plinking sounds came together and assembled themselves into music with chords and crescendos, and I thought that Victoria must be at the keyboard, though I'd never heard her play with such power. I walked into the foyer hallway where the piano was situated, and to my surprise, Will and Maddie were seated on the bench. Victoria was standing in the opening to the sitting room. She and I met eyes, and she smiled and shrugged.

Will stopped abruptly, and Maddie clapped her hands.

She had a thin book—a music book—on the bench beside her. She picked it up and held it toward Will.

"Now," she proclaimed. "Aunt Kara and Aunt Vicki, we're all gonna sing."

The cover of the music book pictured a Christmas tree and elves and big decorative snowflakes.

Victoria joined them at the piano, but I hung back.

"I don't sing."

Will cast a look toward me. "You love music."

"But I don't sing."

He grinned.

"Come. Now," Maddie insisted, waving her hand at me.

"Come and sing now, Auntie Kara," Will said. "We

need you."

It was good to see Maddie animated again. I should be glad to be included—wanted—to have this happening right here in my home. A delicate shiver raced up my body, warming me.

I joked, "Well, if you don't like what you hear, I don't want to *hear* about it. Remember, you asked for it."

Will accepted the music book from Maddie and opened it wide as he situated it against the stand. "This one?" he asked her. "'Jingle Bells'?"

Maddie started singing and laughing all at once, and Will began playing. Eventually we all got caught up on the same notes and words, except for the musical ad-libs Maddie threw in, apparently remembered from other versions.

That night, after Will had left us and Maddie was tucked in and sleeping soundly, I was in the kitchen washing up the last of the dessert dishes. Victoria entered the kitchen with a last, missed dish.

She said, "Need any help?"

"Nope. I've got it."

"Then I'm heading to bed." She paused in the doorway to add, "Just a reminder—that mail I've been getting in and sorting for you is stacking up."

"Thanks for bringing it in for me. Seems like my timing and the mail carrier's delivery schedule never match up. I appreciate you separating the Christmas cards from the flyers and bills. You are far more organized than I realized. I've decided to let the piles grow. I'll tend to them in a few days." I smiled and felt it inside. "The power company isn't coming to disconnect, and our utilities are safe into the new year."

"Doesn't sound like you."

I shrugged. "I'm dancing to a different drummer this holiday."

"Good for you. You might reconsider, though, when it comes to the Christmas cards. They're sort of time-sensitive. If you run into any senders, they might ask if you got their card."

"Really?"

"Possible. Good night, Kara."

"Good night, Victoria."

"One last thing," she said. "In case you didn't already know this—that man is a keeper."

"Will? You're right about that."

She grinned. "You bet I am. And don't look so surprised. Believe it or not, occasionally I do get it right.

CHAPTER THIRTEEN

Friday, December 20 ~
Five Days Until Christmas

The phone rang early the next morning. Nicole was hurried and breathless. Without wasting words, she said Mel was sick and they were headed back to the hospital.

"The doctor is sending us there via ambulance."

"Serious?"

"Seems so. I'll call you as soon as I know." She disconnected.

I clasped my cell phone and held it to my chest.

Should I tell Maddie? It took me a split second to know the answer. *No.* Time enough to tell her later if it didn't work out. If it went badly. Time enough then to ruin Maddie's Christmas. Today was her last day of school and the class party, and then the children's Christmas pageant at the Baptist church this evening. Maddie should be told that Grammy and Nicole wouldn't be there, but she didn't need to know anything else until I had something concrete to tell her. So I dropped her off at school per our plan and kept my worries to myself.

I tried to stay busy performing necessary tasks until it was time to retrieve Maddie from school. I left her coloring in my workroom, but when I returned, she was in the sitting room, cross-legged on the rug. Her chin was propped in her hands, and she was gazing at the stockings we'd hung from the fireplace mantel.

Watching her, warmed by the perfect innocence of her contentment, fascinated by the decorations and imagination and hope, I was glad we'd taken extra effort to make this Christmas special for Maddie. These things, these moments, couldn't be reclaimed if you missed them.

She looked toward me and then away. No joy was in her expression.

"Maddie, what's up, sweetie?" When she didn't answer, I eased down to the floor beside her.

Obviously, she wasn't lost in dreaming of presents and the gaudier parts of the holiday, but to get to the heart of her worry, I asked, "Are you thinking about Santa?"

She shook her head. "No, ma'am."

"Maybe his reindeer? Rudolph?"

"No."

In a softer voice, I asked, "Are you worried about singing in the pageant?" No answer. "Or about Grammy?"

"I miss her."

"I know. I understand. She misses you too."

"I saw her last night."

"Oh?"

"In my sleep. She had a present for me." She stared ahead. "I don't know what it was. She left before she gave it to me."

Not what I was expecting. I repeated, "Oh?" I took her hand, held it, and kissed the back of it. "I have to tell you something that might make you sadder."

She sniffled.

"Nicole called this morning. Grammy isn't feeling so great today. She had to go to the doctor again. We didn't know that would happen, or we would've told you. She'll need to rest extra today, so she can't come to the pageant tonight, and Aunt Nicole and Uncle Seth will want to stay with her."

Maddie said, "I'll stay with her too. I can be a nurse. I can do what a nurse does."

"Oh? That's great. Like what?"

"I can fix soup."

"How? You don't use the stove, do you?"

"Microwave."

"Really? I didn't realize how tall you are."

"A chair, Auntie Kara. I can stand on a chair."

I stared at her with mock solemnity. "Have you actually used the microwave?"

"No, ma'am. But . . . but I could. I know how. And I can fix sandwiches. I have made peanut butter and jelly and bologna sandwiches lots of times."

I sat back, displaying shock. "Peanut butter, jelly, and bologna? Oh, goodness. What kind of sandwich is that?"

She groaned and giggled. "Not all at the same time, silly."

I touched her hand again. "Just seeing you would be excellent medicine, but she needs rest. Plus, who would sing in your place tonight?"

Maddie shook her head. "Grammy is sick. I don't want to sing."

"She would want you to sing. You know that?"

Her lower lip came out, and she didn't answer.

"The choir leader and the other children are depending on you to do your part. Grammy can't be there, but I can record it with my phone, and then when Grammy is feeling better you can show her yourself."

Her eyes shifted as she considered it.

"Okay," she said. "I will."

"Excellent." I waited, thinking. "You know what? It's time for a quick supper and then we'll get ready to go. Did you know that I've never seen a Christmas pageant?"

"Truly?"

"Truly."

She grinned. "Now you will. I'll wave to you."

"Will your choir leader mind?"

She giggled. "Not if I wave small. And it can be a wave to Grammy, too, for her to see later."

"I'll do my best to catch it on the video, sweetheart."

Chapter Fourteen

All day long I'd kept my phone close to me, just in case Nicole called. There were no calls, but I received a couple of texts. They were thin on details. The results of tests and whatever else was being checked and monitored was "encouraging," and in one of the texts, Nicole expressed hope that they might be heading home soon, so we kept moving forward with our plans. I was determined that while Mel, Nicole, and Seth were doing what they had to do, we—Maddie and I—must do the same.

The choirs—from the adult choir to the children's choirs—all performed at the evening service. The songs were interspersed with vignettes of the nativity—Mary, Joseph, shepherds, and wisemen—all played in miniature by the young actors. Despite occasional outtakes by the youngest members of the tableau scenes, every church member and visiting grandparents and aunties and uncles were proud of the young participants. I rarely found myself in church, and I thoroughly enjoyed the feeling of community and love that surrounded me in this celebration. Maddie was one of the many shining faces and eager, intense performers, and yet I saw a special light around her. If my perception of that light was due to nothing more than love, then it seemed too simple, and yet, at the same time, it made perfect sense and was a testament to the value and strength of a human connection that was possible, even for someone like me.

I raised my phone as Maddie's age group took their place center stage, and I focused on the group of twelve children, boys and girls. They kept their eyes solemnly trained on the choir leader directing them. I hit record and tried to hold the phone discreetly without blocking anyone's view. The bell and notification sounds were turned off, of course, but as the children finished their song and filed off the stage, a notification lit up the screen. A text.

Nicole: *Mom's fine. Returning home in the morning. All's well.*

As the last group of children sang the verses of "Mary Had a Baby," I handed the phone to Victoria so she could read the text too. Then I reached up unconsciously to touch my face and was surprised to feel the moisture on my lashes. A woman next to me handed me a tissue and gave me a smile, then turned her attention back to the performance. Nicole's news and a stranger's kindness squeezed my heart, and a tear broke free and ran down my cheek to be captured in the corner of my smile.

After the last group finished singing, the pastor sent us on our way with a blessing. The program had lasted just over an hour. As I stood and turned toward the aisle, I glimpsed a familiar figure a few yards away, half-hidden by the crowd. When he turned to speak to someone—as if offering an apology for cutting them off—I recognized Seth.

I wouldn't yell out. Clearly, he'd been attending covertly. Deliberately avoiding me? It made me sad. Even if he'd been a late arrival, there'd been room to sit with us. Except he hadn't wanted to, for whatever reason. And that made me mad.

"Victoria, will you find Maddie and meet me outside?"

Making my way into the aisle, I snaked through the crowd until I reached the main entrance. I managed to exit outside just as a car—Nicole's car—drove past me. The lamplight showed me there was only one person in the vehicle. He'd looked my way briefly. Had he seen me? He didn't stop or even slow. He just kept going.

I stood there.

Victoria spoke from behind me. "I have our little angel here. She's ready to get home and have a snack. Hot cocoa, I'm thinking."

Seth was a big boy. He'd have to figure this out on

his own. I forced a smile.

"You were wonderful, Maddie. Let's go see about that snack. We'll break open the Christmas cookie. I'm thinking cookies and a mug of cocoa sounds delicious right about now."

~~~~

We were home by eight o'clock, and Maddie was asleep by ten. Not me. I was restless. Annoyed. I'd managed to hide my edginess from Maddie, though Victoria had looked askance at me a few times, likely wondering about my mood. Smart woman, Victoria. Too smart to ask about it, because I was ready to blast someone.

I reminded myself that I should let Seth work out his issues on his own. I shouldn't take his avoidance personally. Whatever was going on in his head wasn't my responsibility.

Maddie wasn't even asking about her uncle—the man who'd been the father figure in her life until only a few months ago, before he'd left for that fancy new life of his on the West Coast. I'd encouraged him to chase his happiness. Well, he'd found it. Did that mean I shared the blame for Maddie losing her uncle?

No, I couldn't take on that responsibility.

What was it that Laura had said the other day when

she'd walked in on Will and me? She'd blushed like fire. I smiled, remembering. After she'd calmed down, she'd said she was certain her brother Lewis would come back into her life if we truly believed and acted on that belief. That we had to be ready to take action when the opportunity arose.

I wasn't sure what to do about Lewis, but when it came to Seth and Maddie I could do my part.

Ignoring how late it was, and that it was dark, I texted him. Since when had I feared the dark at Wildflower House? Never.

Kara: *Meet me at the bridge.*

Seth: *What? You ok? Maddie ok?*

Kara: *Everyone's fine. Meet me at the bridge.*

Seth: *I'll call.*

Kara: *Bridge. It's dark. Bring a flashlight. See you in ten.*

Humph. Satisfied that I'd gotten Seth's attention, I donned my furry boots and my coat, snagged the flashlight from the kitchen, and stepped out to the porch.

The night had a fresh, clean feel. The moon was out, and the stars were bright. I didn't need to turn on the flashlight until I reached the creek and entered the forest. Even then, I could almost have walked the path sightless because I knew it so well, but there were always roots waiting to trip you up.

He beat me there. I saw the bright end of his flashlight dangling at his side as I neared the bridge. I joined him there, but kept a couple of yards between us.

"Is something wrong, Kara? It's been a long day."

He was annoyed? Was that what I heard in his voice? *Really?*

"Is Mel still expected to be released tomorrow morning? She's doing okay?"

"Thankfully, yes. It was a medication issue. They got it sorted out."

"Good."

"What's this about?"

"You—that's what this is about," I said. "Are you avoiding me?"

I expected denial, but Seth could always be relied upon to surprise me.

"Yes," he said. "I suppose I am. I didn't want to complicate your life."

"How would you complicate my life? We went our separate ways months ago. I thought we were still friends."

There was a long silence.

"We are," he said finally. "But . . . you say months. It doesn't seem that long ago to me. I know you and Will Mercer . . . I didn't want to make you or Will feel awkward."

"Or yourself?"

He shrugged and looked away. "Or me."

"Will is fine, and I am fine. And your presence is vastly more important in Maddie's life than anyone's awkwardness."

I might possibly be overstating Will's "okay-ness" with Seth being around, but Will was an adult and even-tempered . . . generally. If Will and I couldn't survive Seth showing up occasionally, then we'd better find that out now.

"I expect you to be at my house tomorrow, Seth."

"I'll see what I can do."

"Nope. Be there. You may not know this, but Maddie hasn't mentioned your name at all. She must know you're here. Maddie talks about everything—except for the deepest, most worrisome things in her life. So be at my doorstep tomorrow as soon as your mother gets home. Nicole can manage after that. Ring the doorbell. Maddie will answer it. Borrow the car seat from me and take your niece out for a jaunt."

"A jaunt?"

"A jaunt. It's a perfectly good word and something everyone should do every so often."

I couldn't see his expression because the moonlight only revealed the sharper structures of his face, but I read a change in his tone, and I seized upon his weakening, forcing it to breathe and grow.

"So be there. Maddie will be ready and waiting."

Seth moved a couple of steps closer to me. "I miss you, Kara."

Once upon a time, I'd desperately wanted to hear those words. But that was then, and this was now.

"We missed you too. Now you can make it up to Maddie Lyn and your mother by not only being here, but by being present for them." I stepped away. "And just so you know, I expect you for Christmas dinner too. You will escort your mom and sister, and we will all share a dinner none of us will ever forget." I added, "Agreed?"

"That will depend on how Mom is doing, but barring anything terrible happening, at least one of us will be there for dinner. For Maddie."

"Thank you."

"I guess I'll see you in the morning then?"

"No guessing about it. Good night, Seth." I turned and walked away. All the stress I'd piled up thinking about whether to confront Seth, magnified by the actual daring of doing it, had activated so much warmth in my body and brain that I was eager to get away, to shed this coat, to breathe again. I heard footsteps.

"Are you following me?"

"Just making sure you get home okay."

"Why wouldn't I? I know the way. No need."

"Yes, there's need. I'll see you home, and then I'll leave." He laughed softly. "Hey, you're the one who insisted I take this midnight stroll through the woods." He added, "I'm sorry you had to do that. I was focused on . . . worried about Mom. Didn't want to deal with anything else."

"Eager to get back to Los Angeles?"

He walked alongside me as much as the path would allow. "True. I like it out there. My job, my friends. But I didn't stop caring about everyone here."

I wanted to lambaste him again about neglecting Maddie, but I'd done what I could. Now it was up to him. "You're staying through Christmas, right?"

"Yes."

"Good."

As we left the woods, he said, "I guess you can manage from here."

"I can. I can manage just fine. In part because you were a friend to me when I first arrived here, Seth. If I didn't properly thank you for that, please accept my thanks and gratitude now. I'll see you tomorrow morning?"

"Yes, ma'am."

CHAPTER FIFTEEN

Saturday, December 21 ~

Four Days Until Christmas

Maddie was restless. We'd made it successfully through the pageant the night before, and this morning, Nicole had already texted that she and Grammy were on their way home.

I was glad Maddie had a lovely distraction arriving a little later.

"Breakfast is ready, Maddie. Come eat. After, you need to get washed up and let me fix your hair. I have a surprise for you."

Her eyes brightened. "What? A surprise? Is it a present?"

"Kind of a present. Mostly just a surprise, but a good one."

While she ate, I went up to her room and laid out a cute skirt and blouse with matching tights. Victoria ducked into the bathroom to braid her hair. Between us, we had Maddie Lyn all bright and shiny and well brushed before the doorbell rang. I looked down at Maddie, saying, "Mind getting the door for me?"

"The surprise," she whispered as she headed for the stairs.

"Be careful! Hold on to the rail!" I followed more sedately.

Maddie screamed, and it hit a note that only an over-the-top thrilled little girl can hit. I was surprised that the window glass didn't shatter throughout the house.

She launched up and forward, trusting her uncle to catch her. He did, and he hugged her and swung her around before falling to his knees. Gently, he set her on her feet.

"I've missed you so very much, my darling Maddie Lyn."

She was still hugging him and refused to let go.

"Maddie?" I said. "How is Uncle Seth going to take you out for a ride if you don't release him?" I looked at Seth. "It's a beautiful day out there. No need to rush back."

I watched them drive away, then dashed upstairs to wrap the last of the presents. Laura was due over anytime now to help. With Maddie away for a few hours, we had to make the most of our time.

~~~~~

About lunchtime, as Laura and I were still wrapping presents, we heard a woman's voice calling out from below.

I stepped into the hallway and looked down the stairs. "Hello?"

Sue Deale appeared at the base of the stairs. "I let myself in. It's cold out there. Hope you don't mind?" But she wasn't waiting for an answer. She'd already walked out of my line of sight, so I started down the stairs. Sue added, "I came across this box while I was decorating."

Now in the foyer, I saw she was holding a large box. It was pretty big, but it must be light because Sue was no burly weightlifter. She'd been the Forsters' relative and heir. Ever since Dad had bought this house and we'd moved in, Sue had been divesting herself of things she couldn't use and "returning" them here to where—she claimed—they belonged. I strongly suspected that her husband, Joe, encouraged her in rehoming the items she'd inherited, and which filled up his attic and garage and shed, and wherever else Sue had been able to fit them.

"Good morning, Sue. Afternoon now, right?"

"Good day either way," she said with a huge smile. "I have a gift for you."

"A gift? Is that box heavy?" I held out my arms.

"Not at all." She passed it to me.

"What is it?"

"Well, let's take a look." She sounded positively gleeful.

Laura had come downstairs to join us. "Hello, Sue!"

Victoria joined us too. I carried the box into the sitting room and set it on Dad's chair to open the loose cardboard flaps.

A mossy-looking roof peeked out from among a bunch of smaller paper-wrapped items.

"I found this when I was pulling out my Christmas decorations. I was going to put it up myself, but then . . ." She shrugged. "I know where it really belongs. And you have little Maddie Lyn here. Christmas isn't the same without a nativity scene."

I'd never had one. Never in my whole life. It hadn't seemed essential in the least . . . but as I was discovering these days, I'd missed out on some important things in my younger years.

As I reached in to lift the wrapped figures out of the box, Laura laid a hand on my arm. "Wait. Have Maddie help you."

She was right. Sometimes a chord is hit in one's heart and brain with such delicate precision that they ring together perfectly attuned, and the resulting note is impeccable in both pitch and resonance.

"Lovely idea. Be careful, though," Sue warned. "It's

a very, very old set."

"We'll be especially careful. I'll bet Maddie is an expert when it comes to arranging the figures in the scene. And where to place the set itself? I'm guessing the foyer table. Have I got that right, Sue?"

"Yes, you do. Mary always displayed it there."

I released the box flaps, and they plopped back into place. I stood in front of Sue, and as I spread my arms wide and moved in for a big hug, surprise showed on her face and she made a soft noise that sounded a lot like, "Oh my."

"Thank you, Sue. Please thank Joe for me too. I wish you both a very Merry Christmas."

"Merry Christmas to you too, Kara."

Sue left. Victoria and Laura went to the kitchen to fix us lunch while I moved the floral arrangement and other items from the top of the foyer table. I set the stack of unopened Christmas cards on the end table beside my chair. I put the cardboard box on the floor beside the table. When Maddie returned, we'd set up the nativity.

Still, I reached inside and pulled out a small figure, carefully unwrapping the paper. A shepherd. I chose another. This one was a lamb. The next was the hay-filled manger.

They were old. So very old.

I turned them in my hands. Were they wood? Or ivory? They were lightly stained with colors. Obviously handmade. Hand carved. So fragile.

But Maddie and I would be careful. I would make sure all the surfaces were covered with towels in case any one of the figures needed a soft landing.

Maddie and I made a good team. With care and love, we'd get the job done.

CHAPTER SIXTEEN

Monday, December 23 ~

Two Days Until Christmas

Midmorning, Seth came by. Victoria and Maddie had gone out to run last-minute errands, and I was alone in the house. Will was working outside. Last time I'd seen him, he was heading out to the carriage house. Some of the bulbs had burned out in the light strings that ran through the trees along the walkway. Those lights would be festive and might even help Santa find his way to us. And in the new year, for evening events, they'd contribute to atmosphere. For now, Will had decided to replace all the bulbs with holiday colors to echo the spotlights on the medallion garden and statue. It seemed like a lot of extra effort to me, but I was fine with it. It made him happy.

When Seth knocked, I answered the door, saying, "She isn't here."

"Good," Seth said. "I hope whatever she's out doing, she's having fun. I came to see you. To apologize."

We stood in the foyer in front of the hundred-plus-year-old photograph of the women who'd lived in this house and attended school here at the turn of the prior century. Seth had found this picture in storage at Sue Deale's house and had given it to me soon after Dad and I had moved in here. Those days—the moving-in days—seemed so long ago, and yet like yesterday.

Below the photograph, the nativity was situated on the foyer table. He stared at the display for several long minutes. "It's beautiful. Looks very old."

"Guess who."

"Sue Deale?"

"Right on the first try."

He laughed softly. "Not too hard to figure out."

"Maddie did the arranging. She couldn't decide whether to group the sheep together and the cows together, or whether to put the lambs and baby cows and donkey together, and then the adult animals in a separate group. We've changed it around several times, but only when I'm right here beside her."

"Is that a plastic goat? It doesn't look like it exactly belongs."

I sighed. "Nope. That's Maddie's. Apparently, she carries it around with her in her backpack. He's a newcomer to the stable."

"Where's baby Jesus? The manger is empty."

"Maddie said he doesn't arrive until Christmas morning. She was very determined about it."

Seth nodded, smiling. "Sounds like our Maddie."

He turned to me. "Things felt unfinished between us. I take responsibility for that—for being absent and expecting everyone would just go on as I'd left them, while I threw myself, heart and soul, into that new life."

He stared at the photo again and then at the needlepoint samplers I'd crafted that hung on either side. "I had to, Kara. If I hadn't focused on the new job and put my whole self into it, I would've drowned. It was incredibly difficult at first. Lots of moving parts. Big expectations from my employers. Having to make it look easy and not show how . . . how scared I was of failing." He faced me. "But that's in the past. The job is still challenging at times, but exciting now rather than intimidating."

"I experienced something similar here at Wildflower House, trying to come to grips with all the changes in my life and always afraid of making the wrong decisions. But I'm surprised you felt that way. You always gave me such good advice when I was struggling. You sounded so confident."

"Easier to give advice than to apply it in one's own life."

I smiled in understanding and sympathy.

He said, "I've always felt that there was some sort of balance—some universal truth—that for anything you gain, something must be lost. Maybe that was the case here." He paused before adding, "I wish you and Will the best. If that's what you want. If he's good for you."

"He is. It feels too soon, though. I worry that I've fallen too quickly. But I'm in love. And I think it may be for the first time. I made it through boyfriends and even a husband and never really understood what love—shared and requited love—was."

"Then I'm happy for you. For you both." He nodded, perhaps finding agreement in his own heart. He cleared his throat. "Speaking of giving, Nicole sent presents over for Maddie since it's looking like she'll be here at least through Christmas Day. She said you were making some additional arrangements gift-wise?"

I nodded.

"A few of them are wrapped and tagged from us already. She said to fit the rest in however you think best. We wanted to be discreet, in case Maddie was around. I'll bring them in now since she's not here."

I walked him to the door. "No need. I can handle it." *Will and I.*

He insisted on setting the packages in the foyer, then he left. I closed the door behind him and went to the kitchen, lost in another world—that of the past—thinking of what we gained and what we lost across the minutes and decades of our lives. As I entered the kitchen, I saw Will standing beside the kitchen table with an odd look on his face.

I stopped. "I didn't realize you were in here." No response. "Seth came by." My heart wanted to lodge in my throat. I coughed to clear it. "Did you overhear?"

He nodded.

"How much did you hear?"

Will moved very close to me. "I heard everything that mattered." He put his arms around me and drew me to him. My face rested on his chest, and I felt his heartbeat against my cheek. "Did you mean it?" he asked.

I nodded. Again, my throat tried to block my speech, but I squeezed out the words. "I do."

We stood there, pressed together, holding each other—afraid to let go, to let this moment move on to whatever might come next for us. But move we did—finally—and when Will kissed me this time, it felt like it might last well into the best future ever.

~~~~~

That afternoon, after Will left and I was still feeling giddy and not wanting doubts or second-guessing to roll in—if they did, I'd be very disappointed—I was standing at the kitchen window and saw a man in the backyard. He was distant, standing down by the creek and near the path entrance.

Immediately I thought of the candy wrapper. The trespasser?

I caught my breath and blinked. When I opened my eyes, he was gone.

He . . . I walked to the back door and out to the porch for an unobstructed view. I had to admit that the figure, obscured by distance and the old glass, had made me think of Dad. Something about his posture or stance?

Wishful thinking. My father would've adored being here with everyone. My father—who'd rarely laughed or cried or shown emotion but who was there for me when it counted—would've adored being here, even now when Wildflower House was an unpredictable hub of comings and goings. Where almost anything was possible. He might've watched more than participated, and our guests might have mistaken his reticence for dignity or arrogance, but he would've loved being a part of it.

A little sad and wistful, I stepped back inside and closed the door.

That evening, Victoria, Maddie, and I sat around the kitchen table and discussed how the prep for the big meal would proceed.

We counted the invitees. Me, Maddie, Victoria,

Will, Will's mom and sister, Aunt Laura, and though I didn't say it aloud, I guessed that Nicole would attend while Seth stayed with Mel. Seven, maybe eight. The dining room table could accommodate that many, especially since one of us was a mini.

After our meeting ended, Victoria and Maddie watched a show on TV while I tidied the kitchen, enjoying the solitude. As I worked, I found I was singing quietly under my breath. *Jingle bells* . . . And I laughed.

~~~~

After I tucked Maddie in and Victoria was reading her to sleep, I stepped outside. The night called to me, regardless of the season. That vast, infinite ceiling of stars and other celestial bodies gave me calm. They existed above like a promise of forever beyond our mortal selves.

I stood at the porch rail where the view was best. I could see the whole sweep of the backyard, the dark forest, and the glittering water. But that lone figure I'd spotted earlier in the day didn't reappear. I supposed I was glad.

Closing my eyes, I breathed in the night like a prayer.

CHAPTER SEVENTEEN

Tuesday, December 24 ~

Christmas Eve

I resolved that we'd have a quiet Christmas Eve at Wildflower House. A peaceful day. No big plans. For this one day we would rest and reflect and enjoy ourselves, because tomorrow would be hectic. Maddie was stretched out on the parlor floor, coloring with pencils. Victoria was upstairs on her work computer. Aunt Laura was coming to spend the night with us to be here for the Christmas morning fun, but she wasn't arriving until later.

The stack of cards that had come in the mail over the last week or so awaited me on the end table. I'd let the cards accumulate, but as Victoria had pointed out the evening before, their senders deserved more respect than that. In fact, I felt rather guilty because I hadn't sent a single card myself. The least I could do was to read these.

I sat in my sitting room chair, propped my feet on the footstool, and prepared to dig in.

Most of the cards were from the folks who'd participated in or attended the Ladies' Auxiliary Holiday Open House. Charming seasonal cards with thoughtful messages. Notes had been written in a few, and I made sure to read each one. I might run into these folks again. I might not remember who sent what, but then again . . .

Near the middle of the stack was a slightly thicker envelope. When I opened it, I understood. Instead of a short note written in the card itself, there was a two-page letter written on notepaper and folded in half, with a small yellowed photo of a young man standing beside a tall cedar tree. The photo had been in color but was decades old. Out of habit, I flipped it over and saw a name penciled on the back. Lewis Martin.

For a moment it felt as if I left reality. My fingers went numb, and the photo fluttered to the floor in slow motion. Buzzing began in my head, and the daylight flowing in through the uncovered windows expanded and overwhelmed me, strangely turning everything dark, and I struggled to breathe. This required decision. Action. I could not, would not, fail here.

I was shaking and shaking, but fingers dug into my arms, pinching the flesh and shaking me more.

"Kara! Kara!"

Victoria's voice. I relaxed. I stopped fighting. Victoria would take control. She was a force. What had she said about that? I couldn't recall. It was long ago and no longer mattered.

My lungs relaxed in one great loss of tension. I gasped in air. My vision was far from clear, and my head was back against the chair, and it was okay. It was okay.

"I'm okay."

"What? Speak louder."

"I'm okay."

"What happened? I walked in and saw . . . I don't know what I saw. You looked like . . . I can't even describe it."

"Photo." I tried to point toward the floor and didn't do it very well, but Victoria understood. She saw the picture and picked it up.

"A picture of your dad, Henry? When he was younger? Did you just find it? Or what?"

As if reading my mind, she fixed her attention on the half-opened stack of cards.

"In there? The Christmas cards?"

I was feeling better by the minute. When she reached toward them, I stopped her, saying, "Read the back."

She did. "Lewis Martin." She looked at me, puzzled. "Lewis?" She sat on the floor abruptly. "Lewis."

And Laura asked, "What about Lewis?"

That snapped me all the way back. Victoria was

staring wordlessly at Laura, who was standing in the foyer, apparently having just entered the house.

"Wait," I said to Victoria. "Just wait." I turned to Laura. "Be patient for a minute. Please. I need to think. Please. Take a seat and let me think." I asked in sudden anxiety, "Where's Maddie?"

Victoria said, "It's okay, Kara. Maddie is asleep on the floor in the parlor. She's worn out with all the holiday stuff." She handed me the photograph, carefully tucking it between my fingers, and then held out her hand to Laura. She urged her toward Dad's chair, and Laura sat, but she was clearly puzzled and concerned.

"You said Lewis," Laura said. "I heard you right, didn't I?"

"I did say Lewis." I held up my hand. "Wait, please. I had a shock, and you may feel the same. Take a deep breath, and then I'll tell you."

"Please, Kara."

"Look at this, Laura, but remember to breathe."

She held it. Her eyes took the slightly faded image apart atom by atom. "Look at the cut of those slacks. I'd guess late eighties?" She glanced up at me, then back down again. "The photo is faded, but clear enough."

I hesitated, wondering why she wasn't seeing what seemed obvious to me, and then I remembered that she'd never met Dad. She'd seen a recent photo of him, but that was very different from a lifetime of living with and knowing someone. "He looks a lot like Dad. Like Henry."

Words attempted to form on her lips. But she couldn't get them said.

"Turn it over."

She shook her head. "No. That's okay." And with great care, she set the photo on the table with the Christmas cards. She stood and walked smoothly out of the room and toward the kitchen.

Victoria stared at me, her mouth agape, and she said, "Crap. She's flown right over the edge to crazy."

I stood, too, but slowly. "Well, if she has, then she's in good company."

"No joke," Victoria said.

After gathering the envelope, the card, and the note, I followed.

Laura was standing at the kitchen sink and staring out the window, but she wasn't seeing anything because her hands were pressed over her face.

"Sit down," I said. When she didn't move, I said it again. "Sit down now, because we are going to read this letter together, and I'm not going to have you fall out and faint or anything else while I'm doing it."

She allowed me to take her by the arm and move her toward the kitchen chair. She didn't resist. I was reassured.

I poured us both a glass of cold water. Clear and

bracing, out of the faucet and straight from the well. I downed several large gulps before unfolding the paper and giving the words a quick scan. I read aloud:

Dear Ms. Hart,

I hope you won't mind me reaching out to you on behalf of my father. He was adopted when he was very young and had very little information other than that he was born in Louisa County and that his mother died. We don't know anything about his father or the birth family. The family who adopted him were from Buckingham County, and that's where he still lives. Knowing he began life in Louisa, he subscribed to the local paper a few years ago. Recently, he saw a newspaper article about Wildflower House and the event held there earlier this month. The reporter wrote a story about it and included some history of the property and also a photo of the house, of you, and of your father, who, according to the article, purchased the house intending to renovate it.

I broke off. I needed to breathe and to think. My chest hurt. I drank more water.

Laura was staring at me. "Stop," she said. "I thought I had faith, but maybe it was no more than hopes and wishes. Suppose he or she is telling us their father is . . . he's . . . gone. Or has dementia. Or that he . . . I don't know. Maybe it's better not to know. To be able to go on hoping."

"I understand exactly what you're saying. I also understand you're talking nonsense. For one thing, this person, I think it's a woman's handwriting, might be totally wrong about the relationship. But we can't live with not knowing when we have the information right here at our fingertips."

"Okay. Skip to the end, then. Go directly to the end and tell me how it comes out."

"Not a chance. Laura, we waited a long time to find each other. We are taking this journey together, and regardless of how it comes out, we are still taking it together."

I shook my head, and a memory stirred. "Nicole mentioned an article would be in the paper. I remember she asked for the photos. Said it would be an advertising opportunity we shouldn't miss. The other day she told me to watch for the newspaper—that they'd be sending me a copy. Maybe they did. I don't know. With everything that's been going on, I forgot about it."

Reassured that I had at least that tiny piece of the puzzle in place, I was ready to continue reading.

Dad and I both noted the resemblance of your father to mine. It is uncanny, really. I was hoping you'd be willing to share information about your family. It may help resolve questions my father has struggled with for years.

I realize this may be a long shot. Dad said (and I do recall him saying this when I was young) that he remembered an older boy named Henry, but not necessarily a relationship. Again, he was very young when he was adopted.

Enclosed is a photo of him when he was a young man. If you are willing to discuss this, my phone number and address are below. I'm happy to talk to you whenever and however you prefer.

Sincerely,

Laura Martin

Laura.

Neither of us repeated the name, but it echoed in our heads at the same time. I knew because I saw what was in my head reflected in my aunt's eyes. Suddenly she was standing and patting at her arms, then her hips, and I understood she was looking for her purse and car keys.

"Whoa. Wait a minute, Laura. You can't go anywhere just now. You *must* calm down."

"I know. I do know." She sat again. "But how can I do nothing? I just missed meeting Henry. Suppose I miss Lewis too?" Her words trailed off in a wail, but it ended abruptly as she got herself back under control.

"I should go check on Maddie. We may have awakened her with our noise. And my phone. I must've left it in the sitting room. When I return, we're going to make a phone call." I took the paper with the information on it. Given how Laura was reacting, I couldn't be sure that it, or she, would still be here when I came back.

"Call her? No, we can't do that. We have no idea who we're talking to or what they might say."

"Like what? You think they might say things we don't want to hear? That we'll be disappointed?" I said as calmly but as firmly as I could. "Laura, please listen to me. I know how much it hurts when you hope and trust and take a chance, only to have it slap you in the face and break your heart. But we've got this. We've got this handled together. Say the word aloud."

"Together?"

"Together." I pointed at the table. "Now wait here. Sit down and take a long drink of that water." I paused in the doorway. "And if you don't mind, cut me a slice of that coconut cream pie that Will's mom made, would you? I need some sugar."

I empathized, and I felt badly for her being so rattled. She was pale. Her eyes screamed panic. Reality and dreams were intersecting, colliding, and it was as scary as heck for her. I understood that. *Been there, done that,* I thought.

Victoria was cuddled up on the sofa with Maddie, watching a TV show with the sound turned up. The background laugh track was good at muffling distant conversations. Victoria met my eyes and gave me a discreet thumbs-up. I nodded and retreated back to the kitchen.

Laura was still there. Seated. A piece of pie was waiting for me. I felt a little nauseous at the thought of eating it. It was delicious and I would eat it, but not at this moment. I drank more water. Holding my phone, I put one finger up in front of my lips as a gesture for Laura to be silent, and then I dialed.

I waited. It rang. And it rang. And went to voice mail. I felt such keen disappointment.

"You've reached Laura. Sorry I can't take your call right now. Please leave a message and have a nice day."

My Aunt Laura now looked less desperate and more curious.

"Hold on," I said. "We'll try again."

Again, it rang until it went to voice mail. This time I had it on speaker so Aunt Laura could hear this woman's voice. When the message had finished, I said, "Hello. I'm Kara Hart of Wildflower House. I received your note, and I'm happy to speak with you whenever it's convenient for you." I gave my phone number and repeated it, then hung up. "So, what do you think?"

Laura said, "I think that maybe her not answering may be a blessing."

"Why?"

"Because I'll feel and sound much more rational after I've had a short time to digest this. I didn't believe it would happen, then I did, but then it seems I stopped believing again. I didn't even know. Now I have to readjust."

I nodded.

Laura continued, "She sounded reasonable, and she even wished the caller a lovely day. I like that. She has nice penmanship and expresses herself well. I feel certain that if Lewis was deceased, she would've said."

"Sounds very logical to me."

"We could drive to Buckingham County," Laura suggested.

"We could, but we won't until after Christmas Day. If we haven't heard back from her by the 26th, you and I are taking a road trip, so keep your calendar flexible."

For the first time since she'd walked in my door today, she smiled. It was the sweet smile of my gentle Aunt Laura.

"Want some pie?" I asked. "I think I can eat it now."

"None for me." She picked up the picture again. "We don't want this to get lost."

"Let's put the photo on the mantel in the sitting

room next to the blue vase. It's a safe place where we can still see it." I added, "For today and tomorrow, we are going to focus on Christmas and saving our sanity."

I dialed the number a few more times that evening, but there was no answer, and soon the voice mail message said it was full.

CHAPTER EIGHTEEN

Wednesday, December 25 ~

Christmas Day

It was barely dawn when I went downstairs. Warm in my comfy robe and slippers, I turned up the thermostat, then lit the trees in the sitting room and parlor. In the kitchen, I switched on the colored spotlights that highlighted the medallion garden and the statue at its center, then the lights that were strung through the trees along the pathway from the house to the carriage house. Lastly, I turned on the light strings on the front porch. They were entwined with greenery and ribbons and looked quite elegant.

Yes, it was early morning, and as the daylight grew the lights would be less obvious, but they would still add a festive, special feeling to the day. Today would be special—as special as I could make it.

As I stood in the foyer, admiring the trees and the mantel decorations, the nativity and the paper cutouts of snowflakes hanging from the ceiling, the silence was broken as Victoria asked softly from above, "Can we come down now?"

Victoria and Laura were poised at the top, each holding one of Maddie's hands. All three were still in their jammies or nightgowns, as was I. It was hard to say which of the three was the most excited.

"Come on down," I said. "Looks like we had a visitor during the night."

Maddie preceded them down the stairs and across the foyer. She stopped just inside the sitting room and looked at the tree and the presents around it. Some of the wrapped presents had already been in place before she went to bed, and now more packages and toys were arranged next to them.

A dish set. A box of princess shoes and tiaras. A fluffy sweater and sneakers that lit up, books, and so on. Everything that could thrill the heart of a young child. Maddie sank to her knees in front of it. The light reflecting off a red glass ball gave her face a pinkish cast. But her hands stayed on her knees, and she made no move to touch the presents, wrapped or otherwise.

"What's up, Maddie?" I should've asked Nicole about the Albers family's Christmas traditions. "It's okay if you want to check out the presents."

She looked up at me, her eyes shining and her face hopeful. "I'll wait for Grammy."

"Are you sure? You don't have to. She wouldn't expect it."

"Grammy will be here today."

"I hope so. I don't know for sure."

"She will." She clasped her hands. "I'll wait."

I cast a quick glance at Victoria and Laura and then gave Maddie a kiss on her forehead. "If that's what you want, then that's fine with us." I felt a little overwhelmed. It was some weird mixture of disappointment and pride—of having had an example set by for us by a five-year-old. I added a little hug, saying, "Would you like breakfast first? Or to get dressed before we eat? We won't have the main meal until one o'clock, so no one will be here much before that."

"Grammy will come." After a pause, she said, "Breakfast. I'm hungry."

"We all are." I stood and offered her my hand. We went to prepare a breakfast fit for a princess—for all of us princesses, regardless of age or kingdom.

~~~~

I made one quick call midmorning, but there was still no answer. After that, I put my phone aside and focused on the coming day. We had lots to do, and I was especially glad to have Laura and Victoria helping. Even Maddie went to work.

I left the front door open so we could enjoy the decorated porch and the morning light through the glass of the storm door. The storm door connected us to the world and was solid enough to keep most of the cold out. There was no chance of snow. The sky was a high bright blue. Not even a puffy cloud was in sight.

The table was set. We'd started it last night, and this morning we added the finishing touches. We'd gone all out, including napkin rings with fake greenery and red cloth napkins. Someone had started Christmas music playing softly in the background. At noon I lit the candles on the mantels and left the matches beside the tall pillar candles on the table.

Victoria gave a soft low whistle at the scene. Laura clapped her hands and seemed barely able to contain herself.

I told her, "I made one more call this morning. Same thing. No answer." I held her hand and gave it a squeeze.

She said, "Tomorrow will be a lovely day for a drive in the country."

"Yes, ma'am, it will."

"Anyone home?" Nicole stepped into the foyer.

Maddie jumped off the sofa and ran for the door.

Nicole grabbed her and hugged her. "Stay back, sweetie."

Between them, Will and Seth ushered Mel up the porch steps. Her color was good—better than it had been for a while.

"You look wonderful," I said.

"Getting there." She pushed away her helpers' hands. "I appreciate you two, but I can manage just fine on my own."

Seth pretended to step back, but he kept his hand on his mother's arm, nonetheless.

Nicole said, "The doctor said Mom could attend if she felt up to it. No big exercise is allowed yet, and she should eat wisely, but the fresh air is good for her."

We turned, hearing a noise behind us. Maddie was trying to drag a dining room chair into the sitting room. Nicole rushed over to save the floor from being scratched.

"Put it there," Maddie said, pointing to a space in front of the tree and presents. "Grammy will sit there."

Part of me wanted to say, *The meal's almost ready. You must wait until after we eat,* but I didn't, and after showing Mel her gifts from Santa, Maddie seemed content to leave the rest for later.

Somewhere in all that I spared a nod and a smile for Seth, and I kissed Mel on the cheek, which made her fuss. Then Vivi and Britt arrived. Will ushered his mother over to meet me. Today was definitely an open-door, walk-right-in situation.

I smiled and took her hand. I wanted her to know I was happy to greet her. Vivi Mercer had reddish hair, cut short, and a pleasant, interested look.

"Thank you so much for coming to share Christmas Day with me. Us."

"Thank you for inviting me. I hope we'll have a chance to chat later. For now, put me to work if there's anything I can do to help."

"We're in good shape, I think. I *hope*." Will's sister, Britt, was nearby, and I said hello to her too before returning to the kitchen.

It worked. It all worked. Between me, Laura, and Vic, we managed to get the meal on the table. There were so many food choices that we had to set some of them on the sideboard. I could've fed several more than the eight already seated around my table. I stood near my own chair. Suddenly, I wanted to just watch the scene for a long moment, to pause it like a Christmas pageant tableau and memorize it. The candles flickering on the table, the scent of green garland, and the lights and glass balls reflecting everything, blended with the delicious aroma of the abundant food filling the room.

"Thank you all, every one of you, for being here today. Mel, I think you are our guest of honor. I am so grateful you came into my life, all of you. None of us got here without a few problems along the way, but we made it." I cast a quick glance at Laura. "We did it separately and yet also together."

Maddie said, "Can I have a roll?"

I laughed. "Yes. Let's eat."

At that moment, the doorbell rang.

The doorbell? Almost everyone I knew walked straight in with a callout at most. A quick scan of the table told me no one was missing—no one who'd been expected.

"You all get started, please. I'll be right back."

~~~~

Reluctantly, I went to the door, achingly aware of the people in the dining room. The rhythm of their conversation followed me as I walked into the foyer and saw her through the storm door glass. A woman with brown hair. She was maybe in her late twenties? She looked reasonable. And without doubt, I knew exactly who she was.

Curious, I opened the storm door, but before I could say hello or welcome, she asked, "Are you Kara Hart?"

"I am. You must be—"

She interrupted. "Is my father here?"

The woman was tightly wound. Anxious. I stepped out to the porch and pushed the storm door closed behind me.

I said, "You must be Laura. I tried calling you. Left a voice mail. Several, in fact. No, your father isn't here. Did you think he might be?"

She seemed to sag. She put a hand to her face and stepped away.

"Have a seat, please. Can I get you some water?"

"Thank you. I'm fine, just discouraged. Dad is so hardheaded. You can't tell him anything. I mean, I'm not trying to disparage him—he has always been there for me, and I love him—but he tends to do his own thing. Always has a good reason, but rarely gives any warning."

"Sounds like my dad."

"Henry Lange? The article said he died earlier this year. I'm sorry."

I nodded. "It took some getting over, but I'm better now."

"When my father saw the article and the resemblance—and finally had a surname—a last name that he could pursue. *Lange*. He wanted to drive here immediately. I convinced him to wait. Or thought I had. We'd already sent the letter, and then two days ago, he just up and left first thing in the morning. Got tired of waiting, I guess, and didn't tell me until after he was gone. He called to tell me he was staying at a local motel and was checking things out before coming to the house. Your house."

"He didn't come here, though I would've been happy to see him. I can't be certain, of course, but I'm pretty sure that my father, Henry, was his older brother. Older by ten years. Dad looked for his younger brother and sister for a long time and got nowhere. He always wondered if the adoption was totally on the up-and-up. He tried to find out but got nowhere."

"I want to hear what you know, but I have to find my father first. I'm sorry I didn't get your call. I was so frantic when I left the house that I grabbed my purse and thought my phone was in it. I was far from home when I realized it wasn't." She waved an empty hand. "I feel almost naked without it." She shook her head again. "I told him—I said, 'Dad, you've waited this long. You can wait a little longer.' I told him we'd find you after Christmas if we didn't hear from you sooner, but he decided he couldn't wait. He must be somewhere in the area."

I remembered the day I thought I'd seen my father— maybe not my father? He'd been down by the creek near the path entrance. For now, I'd keep that to myself. I didn't want this woman, *this new Laura*, running off into the woods to search for him.

"I'm sure you're right. Why don't you come inside?"

She motioned toward the cars parked along the

driveway. "I'm so sorry. I saw the vehicles and knew you must have lots of company, but I couldn't wait."

"No problem. Truly." I wanted to calm her and have a moment to think. "Come in and we'll call the sheriff's office. Other than that, I'm sure he'll show up . . ." I didn't know if I finished that sentence or simply allowed it to die midstream, because a truck caught my attention. It was similar to Will's truck, but not Will's. It was parked in my paved parking area, and despite the pines and bushes between me and it, I saw a tall, thin man standing beside it. Laura's view of the lot had probably been blocked by the vehicles parked along the drive, and by the additional camouflage of the landscaping and the trees.

I took her hand, clearly startling her. I pointed past her shoulder. "Could that be . . ."

And she was gone, quickly disengaging from my hand and hurrying down the steps. The man was already walking our way. His tentative steps grew more confident as his daughter got closer.

Her back was to me, and I think she yelled at him first, but then she threw her arms around his neck, forcing him to stoop while she hugged him. When she let him go, she kept her hand on his arm, and they walked back toward the house, and me.

"Are you okay, Kara?" Laura asked.

Aunt Laura. She was standing on the threshold,

holding the storm door open. I must've looked alone on the porch.

"Can you step out here with me?"

"Of course, dear. What do you need?" She added, "Who's that? Who—?" She broke off with a gasp.

"Breathe, Laura. Stand here and breathe, and I'll greet him." I grinned at her. "Let's not scare him off first thing, okay?"

She patted my arm but didn't speak. I felt breathless myself. He didn't look exactly like my dad, but so close that I almost couldn't bear it.

I walked toward the steps. "Hello. Welcome to Wildflower House and to my home. Are you Mr. Martin? I'm Kara Hart. Your daughter and I are wondering if you might be my father's younger brother?"

He joined me on the porch, his daughter behind him now, and Aunt Laura behind me.

"Yes," he said. "Is it true? I'd given up looking until I saw that photo of Henry Lange." He repeated, but softly, "Lange." His clothing was neat but nondescript. A cotton button-down shirt. Slacks. His posture was perfect, and his hair was cropped rather short. I guessed prior military.

"You look so much like my father that I'd be greatly surprised if you aren't his brother Lewis. I'm sorry you missed meeting him."

"I drove over yesterday but saw people coming and

going, so I left. I came back this morning and saw even more cars and people. I should've guessed it would be that way, being Christmas Day and all."

Lewis was well spoken in a quiet, controlled way. He added, "I apologize for interrupting your holiday celebrations."

"I'm glad you're here. Come inside and join us for dinner. We have plenty."

Lewis stayed put, as if I hadn't extended the invitation. "I vaguely remember Henry. I'm pretty sure it's him that I remember, anyway, but that's about it."

Aunt Laura was still behind me. I felt the tension in her growing and expanding, almost like an electrical field. Any second now she was going to either faint or knock me out of her way. I abandoned any further attempt to ease this man into our reality and said, "You may remember more than you realize."

"Possible. Maybe more will come back."

"You had a sister, too, you know. *Have*, actually."

"I . . ." He sputtered, out of words too quickly.

"A twin," I added. I reached over and pulled his daughter into our circle of conversation. "Laura, I'd like you to meet my aunt. She's my father's younger sister, Laura."

The younger Laura gasped, and Aunt Laura hugged her. Lewis went silent and looked stunned. By now, Will and Victoria had come to the front door, and soon the rest of the guests had migrated to the foyer to see what was going on.

I took Lewis's hand and touched Laura's arm. "Please come inside. Please join us. It will only feel awkward for a moment, and we'll have all the time we need to talk later."

Lewis said, "We don't want to intrude. I never intended to—"

Victoria said, "I've already added the new place settings. We have plenty of room. The food is getting cold." Like a general ordering her troops, she swept her arm forward, toward the interior.

And we went, every one of us.

Later, I tried to sort it out in my memory, but even though we all moved to the dining room as directed, it was a blur until Victoria yelled for attention. She was standing at the far end of the table. Nicole, Mel, and Seth were seated to her right, and the rest of us were otherwise arrayed around the table.

"Kara?" Victoria spoke my name loudly. "Mind?"

She was standing and holding a glass aloft. Her eyes were bright. Her intent expression warned me she had a lot to say and was eager to get it said. My instinct was to intervene. Victoria could be . . . Before I could stop her, a hand claimed mine. Will. I grasped his hand in return and leaned against him. I nodded at Vic and smiled. "Please do."

She raised her hands as if to generally encompass everyone in the room. "Thank you all for being here today. For coming together on this amazing day. This day of miracles."

For a moment, she stopped, a little choked up. Thinking I might need to step in after all, I moved. Victoria signaled me to wait.

"I'm fine," she said. "Everyone, please bear with me while I take a moment to welcome and introduce our newest guests. This is Laura. She is Henry Lange's niece from out of town. And this is Lewis, her father, and Henry's younger brother. This is not the time to go into details—nor to ask questions. Kara, Laura, and I worked hard on this meal. This fabulous meal. For which we are also grateful."

After a longish pause, Victoria cleared her throat. "I am grateful and honored to be here to share this Christmas Day at Wildflower House. Mel—we are delighted that you are recovering and here today. Lewis and Laura—you won't know this, but I belong here less than anyone. I'm not family. At times, I haven't even been a friend. At least, not a good one. But I'm here. And that's another miracle." She raised her glass. "I'd like to toast Kara Lange Hart, our hostess, our friend, and our family, in every way that matters. She hadn't planned on any of this back in the spring, and yet how fortunate we all are that she made it happen. To you, Kara."

Will handed me a glass and lifted his own. Everyone participated, and somehow in that moment of silence and appreciation, chaos warmed into camaraderie.

"Thank you, Victoria. To you, as well."

The meal was an amazing kaleidoscope of curiosity, excitement, and triumph, and of laughter and tears. Mel was with us. Maddie was delighted. Seth paid particular attention to both of them. Somehow Nicole and Lewis had ended up seated side by side. She kept glancing at Lewis with odd little smiles brightening her face. She'd loved my father, and I'm sure she was seeing a slightly younger version of my father in Lewis—a version closer to her own age. Was that good or bad? I didn't know, and it wasn't my business.

Laura and Laura chattered. I caught snippets of their conversation but left it to them, because I was seated near Will's mom. Vivi and I tried to converse, but with all the craziness, our exchanges stayed mostly polite and surface, and I was content with that for now. As the meal was breaking up, I offered her a tour of the house and took that opportunity to speak a few more words with her and to apologize for all the drama.

"All good drama," she said. "Hard to beat that.

Especially at Christmas. I never imagined that I'd witness long-lost twins reuniting before my eyes. Definitely a Christmas never to be forgotten."

I sighed. This story would be all over the county before the sun set today. Dad would've been uncomfortable with that public exposure.

I stopped, surprised, and then I laughed. Too bad this hadn't happened sooner. Maybe we would've found each other all the quicker if Dad had been more open about his life. But he hadn't because he couldn't. Sometimes we just had to be who we were—our own special mixture of flaws and strengths.

Merry Christmas, Dad.

Will had come to stand beside me again. I took his hand. Somewhere under the tree among the other presents was my gift for him and his for me. We would open the wrapped presents later. For now, I had as many gifts as I could handle, and they were all alive and well, laughing and talking around me. My heart—and my Christmas— was full and overflowing.

THE END

ACKNOWLEDGMENTS

Thank you to everyone who contributed to *The Wildflower House* series, including Lake Union Publishing and my editor, Alicia Clancy, who produced *Wildflower Heart* and *Wildflower Hope*, and to my amazing beta readers, Jill, Amy and Amy, who read the unfinished manuscripts, discussed the characters with me as if they are people we know personally and care greatly about, and who offered advice on all three books and brainstormed possible future Wildflower House books with me. Special thanks to editor Jessica Fogleman who used her skills and talents to give *Wildflower Christmas* its final polish.

BOOKS BY GRACE GREENE

Emerald Isle, North Carolina Novels

Beach Rental
Beach Winds
Beach Wedding
"Beach Towel" (A Short Story)
Beach Christmas *(Christmas Novella)*
Beach Walk *(Christmas Novella)*
Clair *(Beach Brides Novella Series)*

Virginia Country Roads Novels

Kincaid's Hope
A Stranger in Wynnedower
Cub Creek
Leaving Cub Creek

Stand-Alone Novels

The Happiness In Between
The Memory of Butterflies

Wildflower House Novels

Wildflower Heart
Wildflower Hope
Wildflower Christmas *(A Wildflower Novella)*

QUESTIONS FOR DISCUSSION

1. *Wildflower Christmas* is a book about healing and reconciliation—both the giving and receiving of it—and about being open to the unexpected, as in, if we're lucky, sometimes we get what we need instead of what we think we want or deserve. What instances do you see of this in *Wildflower Christmas*?

2. Kara had trouble accepting her father's death and being open to new opportunities. She made great strides toward acceptance in *Wildflower Hope*. Do you think she finally resolved the old, unhappy feelings and the newer grief in *Wildflower Christmas*?

3. What about Victoria? She played a strong role in *Wildflower Christmas*. How might the story have been different if Victoria hadn't invited herself to stay at Wildflower House for the holidays?

4. Do you have favorite holiday memories? What about unexpected events? How did they impact your accustomed traditions?

ABOUT THE AUTHOR

Photo © 2018 Amy G Photography

Grace Greene is an award-winning and USA Today bestselling author of women's fiction and contemporary romance set in the countryside of her native Virginia *(Kincaid's Hope, Cub Creek, The Happiness In Between, The Memory of Butterflies, Wildflower Heart, and Wildflower Hope)* and on the breezy beaches of Emerald Isle, North Carolina *(Beach Rental, Beach Winds)*. Her debut novel, *Beach Rental*, and the sequel, *Beach Winds*, were both Top Picks by RT Book Reviews magazine. For more about Grace, visit www.gracegreene.com or connect with her on Twitter @Grace_Greene and on Facebook at www.facebook.com/ GraceGreeneBooks.